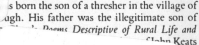

THE PARISH

...s born the son of a thresher in the village of Helpston, near .... ugh. His father was the illegitimate son of the parish clerk. In 182... ..... *Poems Descriptive of Rural Life and Scenery* was published by .... John Keats and other notable writer... ....tion and Clare also published ....827 appeared *The Shepherd'* .... Clare moved to the nearby v .... .tage specially prepared for h ....sper and in 1836 was sufferi... ....tered the private asylum of Matthew .... / as a voluntary patient, but, walking back to Northborough in 184., ne was removed to Northampton Asylum, where he stayed until his death, continuing to write a large body of poetry. In every generation since his death there has been someone who has promoted his fame, but it is only in the last twenty years that he has begun to be widely read. His reputation as a great English poet still awaits recognition by the academic world, but the general reader has ceased to have any doubts of his status. His continuing delusion that he was married to his first girl friend, Mary Joyce, as well as to his real wife, Martha (Patty) Turner, has always added a special poignancy to the story of his life.

Eric Robinson is Professor of History at the University of Massachusetts, Boston, and Vice-President of the recently formed John Clare Society. He has published works on the economic history of the Industrial Revolution and has taken part in television and radio broadcasting in both Britain and the U.S.A. With Geoffrey Summerfield he has edited John Clare's *The Shepherd's Calendar* (1964) and *The Selected Poems and Prose of John Clare* (1967); with David Powell he has edited the Oxford Authors *Clare* (1984) and the first two volumes of the Oxford English Text *Clare* (1984); and he has also edited *Clare's Autobiographical Writings* (1983) and, with R. S. Fitter, *John Clare's Birds* (1982).

David Powell, F.L.A., was on the staff of the Northampton Public Library from 1955 to 1972, where he was responsible for the John Clare Collection. He has edited the Catalogue of that collection (1964), *John Clare, The Wood is Sweet: Poems for Young Readers* (1966) and *Christina Rossetti, Doves and Pomegranates: Poems for Young Readers* (1969). He is now Technical Services Librarian at Nene College, Northampton.

John Clare

THE PARISH
A Satire

edited with an Introduction by
Eric Robinson
and notes by David Powell

Penguin Books

Penguin Books Ltd, Harmondsworth, Middlesex, England
Viking Penguin Inc., 40 West 23rd Street, New York, New York 10010, U.S.A.
Penguin Books Australia Ltd, Ringwood, Victoria, Australia
Penguin Books Canada Limited, 2801 John Street, Markham, Ontario, Canada L3R 1B4
Penguin Books (N.Z.) Ltd, 182–190 Wairau Road, Auckland 10, New Zealand

This edition first published by Viking 1985
Published in Penguin Classics 1986

The Parish: A Satire copyright © Eric Robinson, 1985
Introduction and notes copyright © Eric Robinson, 1985
All rights reserved

Reproduced, printed and bound in Great Britain by
Hazell Watson & Viney Limited,
Member of the BPCC Group,
Aylesbury, Bucks
Typeset in Bembo

Contents

Acknowledgements

Our chief debt is to Peterborough Museum and Art Gallery where our copy-texts for *The Parish* are to be found. We are also grateful to Northampton Public Library, the Carl and Lily Pforzheimer Foundation, Inc., and the Carl H. Pforzheimer Library for permission to quote from manuscripts in their possession, and to the Master, Fellows and Scholars of Christ's College, Cambridge, for permission to quote from letters in the college muniments.

Manuscript numbers preceded by a single capital letter refer to the Peterborough Museum Collection. Those without a capital letter belong to Northampton Public Library.

We also wish to draw the attention of readers to the very valuable services of the John Clare Society, whose Membership Secretary is George Dixon, 8 Priory Road, Peterborough (Tel. 0733 62039).

Introduction

John Clare's fame as a poet of nature and the English countryside grows every day. *The Shepherd's Calendar* has become one of the best-known poems of the nineteenth century and his sonnets, such as 'The Thrush's Nest' and 'The Mouse's Nest', are as celebrated as Bewick engravings. Some of the intense songs of the years of his madness are also popular. But John Clare, the satirist, laughing at the antics of strutting farmers and castigating the hobbies of simpering Victorian misses, has hardly yet reached the consciousness even of those readers who celebrate our 'Honest John'. For this reason we have decided to publish *The Parish*, his major satirical poem, in its fullest recoverable form, so that the reader can see Clare as an acute, if caustic, observer of men and customs as well as of nature. This version dispenses with an elaborate scholarly apparatus but preserves Clare's grammar and diction as he intended them.

Lines 1584 to 1725 incorporate a poem which Clare elsewhere entitles 'The Vicar' and we know, from his letter to his publisher, John Taylor, dated 11 August 1821,[1] that 'The Vicar' was then complete. On the 4 January 1823 Clare claimed that *The Parish* was finished,[2] but on 12 May 1826 he was still talking about improving it.[3] Dating *The Parish* is not easy as parts of it appear in no less than eighteen manuscripts, but much of it was written between 1820 and 1824, with additions probably as late as 1827.

The Parish is fairly early in the canon of Clare's works – his first volume, *Poems Descriptive of Rural Life and Scenery*, was published in 1820 – and therefore written just as he had become an overnight wonder in the literary circles of London, had met

1. J. W. and A. Tibble (eds.), *The Letters of John Clare* (London, 1951), p. 124. This work is about to be replaced by Mark Storey's superior edition (Oxford, 1985).
2. ibid., p. 140.
3. ibid., p. 192.

Coleridge, Hazlitt, Charles Lamb and others, and had married Martha Turner (Patty) and started his family. One might have expected it to be a poem written with some hope and expectation, but that is not so. In many places it is a harsh poem and Elaine Feinstein is right to say that 'In Clare's *Parish* the bluntness, and trenchancy of rhythm and vocabulary suggest an angry man'.[1] Much of the imagery is drawn from the farmyard and the dung-heap:

> A dirty hog that on the puddles brink
> Stirs up the mud and quarrels with the stink   (ll. 319-20)

> A set of upstarts late from darkness sprung
> With this new light like mushrooms out of dung   (ll. 495-6)

> Whose dung hill pride grows stiff in dirty state   (l. 2056)

and Feinstein also points out how the word 'dirty' is used throughout the poem to describe the behaviour of the rich. Clare is explicit about the origins of the poem. It was, he tells us, 'begun and finished under the pressure of heavy distress, with embittred feelings under a state of anxiety and oppression almost amounting to slavery . . .'[2] He opens the poem by defending his own position. He is not, like some sycophantic writers, going to write of myrtle groves growing in winter, nor will he tell us

> That golden showers in mercey fall to bless
> The half thatchd mouldering hovels of distress   (ll. 19-20)

nor that his village is an Eden, to which Eden itself was only a desert, where a beggar is blessed with an Adam's life because he lives under such wise laws. Clare is going to satirize the deceit of the ruling classes in his parish and unmask the cant, hypocrisy and envy of those who are responsible for the oppression of the poor.

One critic, John Barrell, has pointed out that *The Parish* is not concerned primarily with the effects of enclosure in Helpston, Clare's native village, and that even if it were, things were rather

1. E. Feinstein, *John Clare: Selected Poems* (London, 1968), pp. 7-8.
2. A 40-1 facing.

better there than in many unenclosed villages.[1] He suggests that at the time Clare was writing *The Parish* the lowest people might have been marginally improving their lot and that Clare did not find it difficult to get manual work. Rather, the poem has more to do with Clare's *perception* of his lot. In fact in one manuscript, MS 30, the poem is given the subtitle, *The Progress of Cant*, and the poem is largely taken up with the exposure of this vice in different sectors of the village population. It is perhaps by concentrating on this subtitle that we may arrive at a better understanding of Clare's frame of mind. Are there reasons why, just at this moment of his first success, Clare should feel himself called to denounce cant and hypocrisy, a denunciation which recurs in several satirical poems at least until 1841 and which, as in *Don Juan*, contributes to the onset of his madness?

First of all, Clare's situation was severe in 1819 and made worse by his fears that he could not help his crippled father who, after breaking stones to make a poor wage, was about to fall upon the parish and lose the family dwelling, an already reduced part of a cottage. Clare himself had worked as a field-labourer, a gardener, a lime-burner while trying to write poetry and get some of his ballads and songs published. He felt a deep sense of gratitude to his parents and yet could hardly keep his own head above water. Even after the publication of his first book and all the fame it brought him – celebration of his work by well-known reviewers, patronage by Lord Radstock and other aristocrats, acquaintance with some of the literary great – things were not much better. He did manage to pay off some debts and save his parents from the workhouse but he had acquired new responsibilities in a wife and child – heavy burdens for a young man with no settled occupation. The general-izations of the economic historian about improved agriculture, growing rural employment, and the advantages of living in a village more or less owned by the Fitzwilliams, must have made little difference to an ambitious young man still trying to make a living as a labourer and being hauled off from his work by some patronizing magistrate just at harvest time.[2] Conditions, on the average, might have been marginally improving but they were still

1. J. Barrell, *The Idea of Landscape and the Sense of Place, 1730–1840* (Cambridge, 1972), Appendix, pp. 189–215.
2. E. Robinson, *The Autobiographical Writings of John Clare* (Oxford, 1983), pp. 118–120.

bad and Clare was not average. It is even possible that some of his habits, such as writing poetry while on the job, were known to prospective employers. Gossip got worse as his fame widened and there were plenty to envy him for what others thought was better fortune than it was, particularly among the parish 'great' whom he satirizes in *The Parish*. Clare tells us in his autobiography about the insults he had to endure from local magistrates, shopkeepers and farmers. Even so there is an animus in *The Parish* which it is not easy to justify by reference to Clare's external circumstances and perhaps the explanation for it should be sought in a long series of disappointments endured by the poet.

First there was the loss of his childhood sweetheart, Mary Joyce, a loss from which he never recovered. It seems to have been sudden and unexpected and Clare never received any explanation. One evening Mary Joyce said goodbye in the ordinary way and he never saw her again. What he does not mention is that the break-up seems to have coincided with the death of Mary's father, James Joyce senior.[1] The new head of the family would have been James Joyce junior who was his father's principal heir. Perhaps he took a different view of Mary's friendship with Clare or perhaps Mary was so upset by her father's death that she needed time to herself. Clare interpreted the breach as a rejection because he was only a poor boy and she the daughter of a comfortable farmer. He had earlier lost through death his friend Richard Turnill and then, because the boy got a post in the Excise, Richard's brother, John. Since their father was Mayor of Stamford, it seems that, at least while they were children, it was easy for John Clare to mix with the sons and daughters of local farmers. But still, one way or another, he lost his childhood friends and the loss of Mary Joyce and of Richard Turnill was connected with a difference in social status. Recovering from these disappointments, Clare fell in love with Martha (Patty) Turner whose parents would have preferred her to be courted by a local tradesman. When she became pregnant Clare at first allowed local gossip to persuade him that the child was not his and prepared to leave her for ever:

1. *Stamford Mercury*, 7 June 1816: 'Died Last week, Mr Jas. Joyce of Glinton, in the 58th year of his age.'

O rose bud thou subject of many a song
Thy defilements so plain to a view
I love thee but cannot forgive thee this wrong
I hope but too vainly adieu

Resolvd never more to behold thee again
Or to visit the spot where ye dwell
My last look Im leaving on Walkherds lovd plain
A last vow Im breathing – farwell[1]

At the same time he was recording (or writing new stanzas for)
the folk-song which begins 'The dove sits in yonder tree' and
which deals with the loss of a true love. Once again Clare felt
himself betrayed, and betrayed because of his low social standing.
He had also allowed himself to be persuaded by malicious gossip
that Patty had been unfaithful to him so that he was both the
victim of deceit and himself a deceiver, a predicament which he
attributed at least in part to his country neighbours.

Unlucky in love, he had also been unfortunate in some of his
professional aspirations: he had tried to be a lawyer's clerk with
James Bellamy of Wisbeach, the employer of Clare's maternal
uncle, Joseph Stimson, and had been ignored by Bellamy after
one look.[2] From then on Clare took jobs as a handyman, a
gardener, a labourer, a lime-burner and in various manual
occupations, staying in none of them very long and probably
getting a reputation for sneaking off into a hedgeside to write his
verses when he ought to have been working. One can imagine
what the local farmers began to say about him. Then came the
meeting with the bookseller and jobbing printer, J. B. Henson
of Market Deeping, who wanted to publish Clare's poems and
persuaded him to have some subscription leaflets printed at
Clare's expense, increasing the price of them without forewarning
Clare and doing little to publish the poems as he had promised.
Clare probably did not know Henson was a bankrupt or he
would have mentioned it.[3] His disgust with Henson and his relief

1. A 1–53 verso. This notebook was written in pencil and rubbed out. The
transcription is therefore open to doubt.

2. *Autobiographical Writings*, ed. cit., p. 59.

3. *Stamford Mercury*, 30 December 1814: 'The Creditors of J. B. HENSON, late
of Market Deeping, printer, may receive at the office of Messrs Sharpe and
Burrell, solicitors, on or after the twenty fifth day of January, next, a Dividend
of 5s. in the pound, on all debts proved under a Deed of Trust, dated the 20th day
of July 1814.'

at replacing him with the bookseller, Edward Drury, are manifested in the autobiography.[1] It is also ironic to see Henson, along with the Rev. John Mossop of Market Deeping and Richard Turnill of Stamford, a member of the 'Market Deeping and its Environs Association for the protection of Property'.[2] Such a contradiction is the subject of Clare's hatred of double-dealing among the rural middle classes. What has not been generally recognized, however, is that Henson actually appears in *The Parish* as Old Ralph, the Ranters' minister; he seduces a young woman in his congregation, who then turn him out. While one may only guess that Farmer Gee of Helpston lies behind Farmer Cheetum[3] and Henry Ryde, steward to the Marquis of Exeter, behind Farmer Thrifty, we can be certain that Henson is Old Ralph. In Henson Clare found double offence: he was a cheating businessman and a religious hypocrite and therefore typical of

> The parish laws and parish queens and kings
> Prides lowest classes of pretending things (ll. 5–6)

And this was a man who had condescended to Clare, who was very sensitive to condescension.[4] Clare also makes it clear that he had a particular person in mind when writing of Bumtagg the bailiff.[5]

After such a series of disappointments, to return to Helpston from London and be subjected to the Rev. Mr Hopkinson, J.P., of Morton and his wife, and to ignorant shopkeepers who asked him whether he had courted his wife in a pigsty, would be sufficient to arouse anger in anyone, and Clare was quick to take offence. He does not object to the true aristocrats, the Fitzwilliams and the Cecils, from whose hands he received kindnesses, but to the petty officialdom of the village: the local magistrate, the Overseer of the Poor, the doctor, the village politician, the bailiff, the constable and the churchwarden. Was he so hard upon the village official because his own grandmother had been

1. *Autobiographical Writings*, ed.cit., p. 96 *et seq.*

2. *Stamford Mercury*, 14 January 1814 and 5 January 1816.

3. A 1–54: 'Gee is thy name thou prating plodding creature & at thy plough tail gee thy horses still . . .'

4. See, for example, *Autobiographical Writings*, ed. cit., p. 96 *et seq.*

5. ibid., p. 115: 'I felt some consolement in solitude from my distress by letting loose my revenge on the unfeeling town officer in a Satire on the "Parish".'

seduced by one? And what did he think of his own son, John, becoming an overseer in Helpston – if he ever knew about it?[1] From these petty officials he was not himself socially far removed while in education, though not always perhaps in grammar, he was their superior. His resentment of them was probably the fiercer because, had his character been different, he might well have been one of them. To him also they represented the decay of an older and healthier tradition. Clare had a standard by which to compare them – the standard of a Golden Age of true community spirit and mutual aid – however false, historically, that standard was.

John Barrell claims that the charges made by Clare against the new farmers are 'conventional ones in the tradition of rural literature of protest', that 'The Parish may certainly speak to us about the "new order which had succeeded the old", but it does not speak about it very directly', and that when Clare offers 'to be specific, the only language he can find is the language of tradition'.[2] In so far as I can understand him, he seems to be saying that Clare's satire is not sufficiently forceful because the standard of comparison by which Clare's farmers are judged is a traditional nostalgic Golden Age which never existed. Barrell, however, seems to have little comprehension of what Clare's Eden meant for him, and suggests that Eden is not a sustained metaphor throughout Clare's creative life and that it is not closely worked into his apprehension of love and innocence wherever he sought for it. But when, at the beginning of The Parish, Clare complains about those false poets who pretend

> That edens self in freedoms infant sphere
> Was but a desert to our Eden here
> That laws so wise to choke the seeds of strife
> Here bless a beggar with an Adams Life (ll. 21–4)

he allies The Parish to all the poems of his long creative life where the traditional Golden Age and the Fall are absorbed into his personal experience. More than most other writers, Clare reinforces his vision throughout a *series* of poems in which the *personal* and the *social* experience are made to strengthen and

1. Photocopy of Retail Beer and Cider Licence issued to John Clare, junior, of Royal Oak Cottage, 1850, in the possession of Eric Robinson.
2. Barrell, op. cit., pp. 198–201.

clarify each other.[1] It is noticeable that when Clare writes about his Golden Age of village life, as in the prose essay 'The Farmer and the Vicar', he often refers to ballad and folk-song which help him to make precise for himself, and for us, if we were sufficiently attuned, a culture in which all ranks of society share a common endeavour and a common enjoyment. Thus, in *The Parish*, the archetypal folk-hero, the Tyburn victim, is opposed, as in Gay's *The Beggar's Opera*, to the deceitful petty official:

> The rogue thats carted to the gallows tree
> Is far more honest in his trade then thee   (ll. 39–40 cf. ll. 1328–9)

while the farmer's daughter, before she has been corrupted by fashion, sings her old songs like the ploughboy,[2] thus celebrating the old ballads of true and false love, of Robin Hood and of derring-do, not drawing-room ballads which were to become fashionable at a later date.

Elaine Feinstein rightly calls *The Parish* 'one of the fieriest political poems in the language'.[3] In its denunciation of Bumtagg the bailiff,

> The worshipper and Demon of despair
> Who waits and hopes and wishes for success
> At every nod and signal of distress   (ll. 2077–9)

followed by his 'lurcher' assistant, and of the parish clerk, master of the stocks and the handcuffs, clapping the brand on the pauper's goods and stirring up trouble at the village dances, *The Parish* carries the conviction of one who has *seen* the poor oppressed, who has *heard* the poor rate being announced in church after the parson's sermon and *watched* the parish clerk

> . . . carrying the parish book from door to door
> Claiming fresh taxes from the needy poor   (ll. 1282–3)

or summoning the parish vestry to reassess the rate.

It has been suggested that Clare is confused when talking about

1. J. Todd, *In Adam's Garden* (University of Florida, 1973), undertakes an analysis along these lines for Clare's poetry up to 1841, but it is applicable to Clare's poetry at all dates. See also *The Parish*, ll. 609–14, 632–6.

2. G. Deacon, *John Clare and the Folk Tradition* (London, 1983).

3. Feinstein, op. cit., p. 10.

the workhouse in Helpston,[2] because, at ll. 1692–3 (in our version), he says:

> Ere mockd improvments plans enclosed the moor
> And farmers built a workhouse for the poor

while at l. 1589 he speaks of 'parish huts' and at l. 1813 refers to the workhouse as a 'mouldering shed', which does not suggest a new building. But l. 1589 does not refer to the workhouse but to the ordinary dwellings of the poor, miserable enough in themselves, while the lines preceding l. 1813 give, it ought to be acknowledged, a most precise account of the workhouse:

> Shoved as a nusiance from prides scornfull sight
> In a cold corner stands in wofull plight
> The shatterd workhouse of the parish poor
> And towards the north wind opes the creaking door
> A makeshift shed for misery – no thought
> Urgd plans for comfort when the work was wrought
> No garden spot was left dull want to cheer
> And make the calls for hunger less severe . . .
> The light of day is not alowd to win
> A smiling passage to the glooms within
> No window opens on the southern sky
> A luxury deemd to prides disdainful eye . . . (ll. 1788–1895 *et seq.*)

The workhouse may be relatively new but it is a 'makeshift shed' and 'Twas not contrived for want to live but dye', which explains why, though recent, it is mouldering. Is it, in any event, credible that Clare would not be well informed about Helpston workhouse? On the contrary, everything in the poem regarding the poor reeks of accuracy.

The Parish or The Progress of Cant is at its best when satirizing religion. Like a child who attends each new church in the weeks before the Sunday School outing, Clare was familiar with several of the religious denominations in his neighbourhood. It is claimed that in his youth, as early as 1814, he regularly attended the Independents in Helpston,[2] while as a child he was reared as an Anglican. In the 1820s he attended both Wesleyan Methodist and Primitive Methodist (or Ranter) meetings. He was interested

1. Barrell, op. cit., pp. 195–6.
2. J. W. and A. Tibble, *John Clare: His Life and Poetry* (London, 1956), p. 33.

in Unitarians and Quakers and even has something to say, from time to time, about Catholics, Jews and Mahometans. His library contained several religious books[1] and religious works are often referred to in his manuscripts. Clare's simple statement, reported by Oliver Gilchrist in *Drakard's Stamford News*, 7 January 1820, that 'My father was brought up in the communion of the church of England, and I have found no cause to withdraw myself from it', is only part of the truth. There is no question that the Church of England was central to his religious belief in his early years (though it seems to be weaker during the Northampton period) nor that Clare was basically a traditionalist, reared in a suspicion of the sects and of enthusiasm in religion. But he was also genuinely tolerant of others' beliefs provided that they in turn were not intolerant. He was a Christian first and an Anglican second. He wanted to see all Christians united in a common faith practising kindliness and love to those in need, whatever their race or creed.[2] Though he had read and studied his Bible carefully, making many verse paraphrases of favoured psalms,[3] he mocked those who searched the Bible for arcane information[4] or who would read no book but the Bible.[5] He disliked strict Sabbatarianism whether practised in the Church of England or in Dissent; he liked behaviour in church to be attentive and reverent but hated a show of religion; and above all he detested hypocrisy wherever he encountered it.[6] One might imagine from *The Parish* that Clare, like his 'old Vicar' in 'The Cottager' was 'down right and orthodox', suspicious of all who

> . . . cant and rave damnations threats by fits
> Till some old farmer looses half his wits   (ll. 523–4)

1. D. Powell, *Catalogue of the John Clare Collection in Northampton Public Library* (Northampton, 1964), pp. 23–34.

2. 'A religion that teaches us to act justly to speak truth & love mercy ought to be held sacred in every country – & what ever the differences of creeds may be in lighter matters they ought to be overlookd & the principle respected' (B 4–136).

3. See, for example, E. Robinson and D. Powell, *The Later Poems of John Clare*, 2 vols. (Oxford 1984), pp. 131–9.

4. *Autobiographical Writings*, ed. cit., p. 74.

5. 'the bigotted assertion that every thing that is nessesery is found in the scriptures' A 46–82.

6. One of his characters says: 'if the last age be censured for open licentiousness this may as justly be condemned for private cant and hypocrisy' (B 4–127).

In *The Parish* solid religion is represented by the *old* vicar, not the *new*, so that it is the Golden Age of the church as well as of the farm that Clare reveres: the old vicar is unpretentious, charitable, lives in a house alongside those of his parishioners, neither hunts nor shoots, keeps the parish in order and behaves, in general, as an amiable eccentric. Such a position would no doubt have been acceptable to most of Clare's patrons, such as Lord Radstock and Mrs Emmerson, if they had seen the poem. Other friends, such as Oliver Gilchrist and the Rev. Mr Holland, would have known that *The Parish* is far from telling all about Clare's religion.[1] In 1824, when *The Parish* was still being composed, Clare was suicidal and in a state of religious turmoil. In a letter of 20 April 1824, he tells his publisher, John Taylor, of his distaste for religious hypocrites but goes on to say that, nevertheless, he has 'determind to assosiate' with 'methodists' in his neighbourhood.[2] In August of the same year he writes to Hessey, Taylor's partner,

> I have found the Ranters   that is I have enlisted in their society
> they are a set of simple sincere & communing christians with more
> zeal than knowledge earnest & happy in their devotions   O that I
> could feel as they do but I cannot

He describes how profoundly their emotional religion affects him. How then do we account for Clare's savage condemnation of both Wesleyan Methodists and Primitive Methodists in *The Parish*?

> The dru[n]ken cobler leaves his wicked life
> Hastes to save others and neglects his wife   (ll. 499–500)

> Thus creeds all differ yet each different sect
> From the free agents to the grand elect
> Who cull a remnant for the promised land
> That wear heavens mark as sheep their owners brand
> Each thinks his own as right and others wrong
> And thus keeps up confusions babel song   (ll. 539–44)

> A set of upstarts late from darkness sprung
> With this new light like mushrooms out of dung   (ll. 495–6)

In addition, the denunciation of 'old Ralph', to which we have

1. See Mark Minor, 'John Clare and the Methodists: A Reconsideration', *Studies in Romanticism*, 19 (Spring 1980), pp. 31–50.

2. Unlike Minor, I take these to be Primitive Methodists.

referred earlier in this Introduction, is one of the most powerfully destructive portraits in the poem. Is it Clare's need for greater religious certainty than he possessed which impels him towards the rather polarized position he adopts in *The Parish*?

Clare's early poem, 'The Vicar', totally incorporated in *The Parish*, creates an idealistic picture of an earlier vicar in Helpston. How historical a picture this is is impossible to determine, but it should be said that conditions for the clergy in Clare's village had not been ideal. In an earlier age, the minister at Helpston complained to Christ's College, Cambridge, about the lessee of the rectorial tithe who allowed swine to be kept in the churchyard. In addition:

> Tis certain the Chancel is much out of repair, and lys shamefully; part of the Ceiling being fallen down, and ye rest is very bad, so y^t dust and pigeon dung falls as oft as there is a wind, and the windows likewise are broke. So y^t ye snow blow in upon us at ye Communion at Christmas.[1]

In 1824, while Clare was composing *The Parish*, Lord Milton was trying to purchase the advowson of the church from Christ's College in order that his father, Lord Fitzwilliam, might improve the living:

> You are of course aware that the College are seized of the advowson of the living and also of the rectorial tythes, which have long been on lease to our family – this separation of the tythes from the living has reduced the income of the incumbent to a very low ebb, the gross receipts amounting as well as I can recollect . . . to no more than 54£ per Annum: In consequence of the penury of the living, there has not been in my memory, nor, I believe, in my father's, a resident clergyman, and perhaps this has been the cause of the immorality & lawlessness of the population.[2]

The parson at Helpston probably resided at Etton, a neighbouring village, until, in 1826, the situation of the new vicar was greatly improved by grants from Queen Anne's Bounty and from Lord Fitzwilliam. That improvement in the parson's own lot, however,

1. Thos. Smith (Helpston) to the Rev. Mr William Towers, Master of Christ's College in Cambridge, 28 January 1727: Christ's College Muniments.
2. Lord Milton (Marske near Gisbro') to the Rev. John Kaye, Master of Christ's College, Cambridge, 29 October 1824: Christ's College Muniments.

may have served, as Clare suggests, to distance him further from his poor parishioners.

The Parish actually emerges from a whole mass of writing about religion, both in prose and poetry, most of which has never been published. In that material it is possible to obtain a more reliable view of Clare's beliefs. A prose passage such as the following roughly corresponds to the traditionalist orthodox Anglican Clare whom we find in *The Parish*:

> & it is with religion as it is with every thing else   its extreames are dangerous & its medium is best – enthusiasm begins in extravagance degenerates into cant & hides at last into hypocrisy   I have reflected long on the subject & find at last as I thought at first that the prayer book contains prayers that are inimatable & that as better cannot be written it is not expected that better can be uttered from extemporaneous prea[c]hers . . .[1]

Here the words, 'at last as I thought at first', should be noted. Elsewhere, as in history on the Bone and Cleaver Club, Clare can reflect critical views of the Church of England ('& the pulpits Mr President I say the pulpits ecchoed with the justice of war & the justice of taxes'[2]) and can find deceitful behaviour in its devotees as well as among the sectarians.

Clare is also, perhaps unfairly, critical of George Crabbe, whose poems in *The Village* were, at least in part, a model for *The Parish*, critical because Crabbe was an Anglican clergyman. How far Clare knew Crabbe's earlier personal history is doubtful, but referring to him he says to Taylor:

> – in our 4 Vol I mean to have a good race with him & have consciet enough to have little fears in breaking his wind – when I read anything that gives me a hint I throw the book down & turn to it no more till mine's finished if thats imitating whats to be said of Milton Dryden Pope &c &c the Boast of English literature – whats he know of the distresses of the poor musing over a snug coal fire in his parsonage box – if I had an enemy I coud wish to torture I woud not wish him hung nor yet at the devil my worst wish shoud be a weeks confinement in some vicarage to hear an old parson & his lecture on the wants & wickedness of the poor & consult a remedy or a company of marketing farmers thrumming over politics in an alehouse or a

1. A 51–11 R.
2. A 46–62.

visionary methodist arguing on points of religion either is bad
enough & I know not which is the best —[1]

The Parish, though it is at its most powerful in the discussion
of religion, might be stronger still if it more adequately reflected
the uncertainties and tensions in Clare's own mind. How far,
one wonders, did Clare simplify his attitude to accommodate his
Evangelical patrons? Clare prided himself on being outspoken
but he was shrewd enough to know that outspokenness was not
always politic, especially for an agricultural labourer with a
family to feed. As it was, *The Parish* never saw the light of day
during his lifetime. Clare knew better than to take on the
Establishment single-handed and the restraint he was obliged
to impose on himself may have contributed to his final mad-
ness.

What were Clare's models for *The Parish*? It should not be
imagined that even at an early date he had not read Donne,
Dryden, Pope, Gay, Swift and many others. Byron was a
particular favourite and Clare was a champion of Pope at a time
when Pope was in disfavour.[2] So with these, and with Crabbe's
The Parish Register, he was not without models. Large portions
of *The Parish*, however, are not satirical and these derive from
the eighteenth-century tradition of descriptive verse. He was
much taken, for example, by the section on the 'Parish priest' in
Goldsmith's 'The Deserted Village'.[3]

It is surprising how accomplished in different verse-forms he
was so early in his writing career. The rhyming couplet was
certainly no stranger to him and several early poems such as 'The
Cottager' (A 41–63) and 'The Haunted Pond' (7–43) are written
in that measure. The concentration on Clare as a writer of
sonnets, songs and ballads has tended to shift the emphasis away
from his use of the rhyming couplet, but he was proficient in it
and used it with some sophistication both in descriptive verse
and in satire. In *The Parish* his power of compression is often
considerable:

> To Gretna green her visions often fled

1. *Letters*, ed. cit., p. 75, Clare to Taylor (1820).
2. 'I have just finished reading the works of Pope & I am astonished at the false
positions of Criticism & taste that I have read about him . . .' (A 18–224).
3. A 3–32.

And rattling coaches lumberd in her head   (ll. 221–2)

The couplet is an epitome of a social history still largely unwritten. Was it Clare's experience of Vauxhall Gardens that enabled him to write:

> His mask is but of lawn and every space
> Lets in new light to show cants crimping face   (ll. 323–4)

Pope could not have improved on that couplet where the implications of the smoothness in 'lawn' are caught up in the deceitful convolutions of 'crimping'. Clare's description of the farmer's booby son:

> Young farmer Bigg of this same flimsey class
> Wise among fools and with the wise an ass
> A farming sprout with more then farmers pride
> Struts like the squire and dresses dignified   (ll. 239–42)

absurdly concentrates on that 'sprout' which is then taken up by 'Struts' in the next line. Clare's ungrammatical 'dignified' also seems appropriate to the character here. Clare's satire is always most vigorous when its objects are closest to Clare's own experience. He is at his best in his detestation of parish tyrants and of parochial hypocrisy. He does not have the sophistication of Pope but he hands out many a good drubbing. The gusto of his satire adds still another dimension to his poetic accomplishment.

Clare undoubtedly felt that he could not afford to alienate either the middle-class professional men, such as Edward Drury and John Taylor, or the gentry, such as the Fitzwilliams and Lord Radstock, who, in their different ways, were promoting his literary career and his material welfare. He was also quite alert to the power of the Anglican clergy, especially in rural England. Beneath the prose note which precedes *The Parish* (see p. 27), there is a passage written in pencil which has been almost completely erased and is therefore very difficult to read. It seems to be apologetic and may include the words 'in the hopes to praise were I could & were I could not have described' and a reference to 'passage contrary to religion laws & morallity'.[1] But even if this should prove not to be an apology there is unmistakable evidence of Clare's writing passages of verse and prose in

1. A 40 – facing p. 1.

Drakard's Stamford News, the radical newspaper of the locality in Clare's time, criticizing the behaviour of gentry, clergy, and even ordinary village people. These passages are unsigned but certainly by Clare and suggest that Clare probably felt that his contributions to a radical newspaper had better go in without his signature. The element of secrecy was undoubtedly present in him and in later years he often contributed quite innocuous pieces to journals under a pseudonym, but in the 1820s self-protection must have been uppermost in his mind. This previously unrecognized poem in *Drakard's Stamford News* of 20 July 1821 represents the same spirit as is to be found in *The Parish*:

Rich and Poor; Or Saint and Sinner

The rich man's sins are under
The rose of wealth & station
  & escape the sight
  Of the childern of light
Who are wise in their generation

But the poor mans sins are glaring
In the face of all ghostly warning
  He is caught in the fact
  Of an overt act
Buying greens on a Sunday morning

The rich man has a kitchen
Wherein to cook his dinner
  But the poor man who would roast
  To the bakers must post
& thus he becomes a sinner

The rich man has a cellar
& a ready butler by him
  The poor man must steer
  For his pint of beer
Where the saint is sure to spy him

The rich mans open windows
Hide the concerts of the quality
  The poor can but share
  A crackd fiddle in the air
Which offends all sound morality

The rich man is invisible
In the crowd of his gay society
    But the poor mans delight
    Is a sore in the sight
& a stench in the nose of piety

Eric Robinson

A Note on the Text

Our text is taken from Clare's fair copy of *The Parish*, to be found in A 40–1/19. Ll. 853–4 and 1906–7 are omitted from our copy-text and have been restored from B 3–28 and A 21–81 respectively. Also omitted from A 40 are ll. 2128–82 concerning Mr Puff. These are taken from A 31–29/29a and are untitled. We cannot be sure that we have placed them in the right sequence nor even that Clare intended them for *The Parish* at all. None the less we feel that we have found a suitable home for them in the Clare canon.

We have made the minimum of alterations to our copy-text. The occasional letter or word in square brackets has been supplied from an alternative Clare manuscript. If a word has been written twice in error we have printed it only once. We have not kept Clare's ampersands. We present Clare's punctuation (or lack of it) and spelling without excuse, correcting only the occasional slip of the pen and a few of the more puzzling spelling irregularities at the following line numbers: 57 its (*corrected to* his), 77 betrays, 299 games, 464 whole (*corrected to* a hole), 483 need (*corrected to* read), 582, 584, 595, 619, 630 preyd, 610 heard (*corrected to* hard), 636 he (*corrected to* she), 692 Doctir, 841 meet, 860 curshed, 876 almosts, 1014 polotics, 1016 poloticians, 1338 hime (*corrected to* him), 1780 preying, 1813 fingure, 2100 white (*corrected to* wight).

In all other particulars the reader can be assured that he is reading Clare's lines exactly as he wrote them. Our full editorial apparatus will appear in the Oxford English Texts series.

Clare's Prefatory Note

This poem was begun & finished under the pressure of heavy distress with embittred feelings under a state of anxiety & oppression almost amounting to slavery – when the prosperity of one class was founded on the adversity & distress of the other – The haughty demand by the master to his labourer was work for the little I chuse to alow you & go to the parish for the rest – or starve – to decline working under such advantages was next to offending a magistrate & no oppertunity was lost in marking the insult by some unquallified oppression – but better times & better prospects have opened a peace establishment of more sociable feeling & kindness – & to no one upon earth do I owe ill will[1]

1. The section of this passage beginning 'but better times . . .' is never quoted and so the reader is left with a more severe impression than Clare intended.

THE PARISH

A Satire

*'No injury can possibly be done, as a nameless character can
never be found out but by its truth and likeness'*

– POPE[1]

The Parish hind oppressions humble slave
Whose only hopes of freedom is the grave
The cant miscalled religion in the saint
And Justice mockd while listning wants complaint
The parish laws and parish queens and kings
Prides lowest classes of pretending things
The meanest dregs of tyrany and crime
I fearless sing let truth attend the ryhme
Tho now adays truth grows a vile offence
And courage tells it at his own expence   10
If he but utter what himself has seen
He deals in satire and he wounds too keen
Intends sly ruin by encroached degrees
Is rogue or radical or what you please
But shoud vile flatterers with the basest lies
Attempt self interest with a wished disguise
Say groves of myrtle here in winter grow
And blasts blow blessings every time they blow
That golden showers in mercey fall to bless
The half thatchd mouldering hovels of distress   20
That edens self in freedoms infant sphere
Was but a desert to our Eden here
That laws so wise to choke the seeds of strife
Here bless a beggar with an Adams Life
Ah what an host of Patronizers then
Woud gather round the motley flatterers den
A spotted monster in a lambkins hide
Whose smooth tongue uttered what his heart denied
Theyd call his genius wonderous in extream
And lisp the novel beautys of his theme   30
And say twas luck on natures kinder part
To bless such genius with a gentle heart
Curst affectation worse then hell I hate
Thy sheepish features and thy crouching gait

1. From Pope's 'Advertisement' to his 'Epistle to Dr Arbuthnot'.

Like sneeking cur that licks his masters shoe
Bowing and cringing to the Lord knows who
Licking the dust for each approving nod
Were pride is worshiped like an earthly god
The rogue thats carted to the gallows tree
40   Is far more honest in his trade then thee
Thy puling whine that suits thy means so well
Piteous as chickens breaking thro its shell
That rarely fails to ope the closest purse
Is far more rougish then the others force
I dread no cavils for the clearest sink
When ere the bottoms stirred is sure to stink
So let them rail I envye not their praise
Nor fear the slander stung deciet may raise
Let those who merit what the verse declares
50   Choose to be vexd and think the picture theirs
On Lifes rude sea my bark is launched afar
And they may wish the wreck who dread the war
Then waves in storms their spite is nothing more
That lash rage weary on a heedless shore
A public names the shuttle cock of fame
Now up then down as fashion wills the game
At whom each fool may cast his private lie
Nor fears the scourge of satires just reply
While those who rail may do what deeds they list
60   They hide in ignorance and are never missed
Their scorn is envys imp conscieved by hate
That tortures worth in every grade and state
As mists to day as shadows to the sun
These stains in merits welfare ever run
Diseases that infect not but at last
Die of their own distempers and are past
Such friends I count not and such foes disdain
Their best or worst is neither loss nor gain
Friendship like theirs is but the names disgrace
70   A mask that counterfiets its open face
Cant and hypocricy disguise their ways
Their praise turns satire and their satire praise
Good men are ever from such charges free
To prove them friends is praise enough for me

Satire should not wax civil oer its toil
Tho sweet self interest blossoms on the soil
Nor like a barking dog betray its trust
By silence when the robber throws his crust
Till fear and mercey all its wrath divides
To feeble portraits buttered on both sides   80
Ill strive to do what flattery bids me shun
Tell truth nor shrink for benefits to none
Follys a fool that cannot keep its ground
Still fearing foes and shewing were to wound
A jealous look will almost turn her sick
And hints not meant oft gauls her to the quick
And hide or shuffle or do what she will
Each mask like glass reflects the picture still
As powder kindles from the smallest spark
Confusion buzzes and betrays the mark   90
From such frail scources every fact is drawn
Not sought thro malice or exposed in scorn
But told as truths that common sense may see
How cants pretentions and her works agree
I coud not pass her low deceptions bye
Nor can I flatter and I will not lye
So satires Muse shall like a blood hound trace
Each smoothfacd tyrant to his hiding place
Whose hidden actions like the foxes skin
Scents the sly track to were they harbour in   100
And each profession of this Parish troop
Shall have a rally ere the hunt be up
To none that rules I owe nor spite nor grudge
How just the satire he who reads may judge

    That good old fame the farmers earnd of yore
That made as equals not as slaves the poor
That good old fame did in two sparks expire
A shooting coxcomb and a hunting Squire
And their old mansions that was dignified
With things far better then the pomp of pride   110
At whose oak table that was plainly spread
Each guest was welcomd and the poor was fed
Were master son and serving man and clown

Without distinction daily sat them down
Were the bright rows of pewter by the wall
Se[r]ved all the pomp of kitchen or of hall
These all have vanished like a dream of good
And the slim things that rises were they stood
Are built by those whose clownish taste aspires
120   To hate their farms and ape the country squires
The old oak table soon betook to flight
A thing disgusting to my ladys sight
Yet affectations of a tender claim
To the past memory of its owners name
Whose wealth prides only beauty stood her friend
And bought a husband that same wealth to spend
Laid it aside in lumber rooms to rot
Till all past claims of tenderness forgot
Bade it its honourable name resign
130   Transformed to stable doors or troughs for swine
Each aged labourer knows its history well
And sighs in sorrow like sad change to tell
The pewter rows are all exchanged for plate
And that choice patch of pride to mark them great
Of red or blue gay as an harlequin
The livried footman serves the dinner in
As like the squire as pride can imitate
Save that no porter watches at the gate
And even his Lordship thought so grand before
140   Is but distinguished in his coach and four
Such are the upstarts that usurp the name
Of the old farmers dignity and fame
And weres that lovley maid in days gone bye
The farmers daughter unreserved tho shye
That milked her cows and old songs used to sing
As red and rosey as the lovely spring
Ah these have dwindled to a formal shade
As pale and bed rid as my ladys maid
Who cannot dare to venture in the street
150   Some times thro cold at other times for heat
And vulgar eyes to shun and vulgar winds
Shrouded in veils green as their window blinds
These taught at school their stations to despise

And view old customs with disdainful eyes
Deem all as rude their kindred did of yore
And scorn to toil or foul their fingers more
Prim as the pasteboard figures which they cut
At school and tastful on the chimney put
They sit before their glasses hour by hour
Or paint unnatural daubs of fruit or flower   160
Or boasting learning novels beautys quotes
Or aping fashions scream a tune by notes
Een poetry in these high polished days
Is oft profained by their dislike or praise
Theyve read the Speaker till without a look
Theyll sing whole pages and lay bye the book
Then sure their judgment must be good indeed
When ere they chuse to speak of what they read
To simper tastful some devoted line
As somthing bad or somthing very fine   170
Thus mincing fine airs misconcieved at school
That pride outherods and compleats the fool
Thus housed mid cocks and hens in idle state
Aping at fashions which their betters hate
Affecting high lifes airs to scorn the past
Trying to be somthing makes them nought at last
These are the shadows that supply the place
Of farmers daughters of the vanished race
And what are these rude names will do them harm
O rather call them 'Ladys of the Farm'   180

   Miss Peevish Scornful once the Village toast
Deemd fair by some and prettyish by most
Brought up a lady tho her fathers gain
Depended still on cattle and on grain
She followd shifting fashions and aspired
To the high notions baffled pride desired
And all the profits pigs and poultry made
Were gave to Miss for dressing and parade
To visit balls and plays fresh hopes to trace
And try her fortune with a simpering face   190
And now and then in Londons crowds was shown
To know the world and to the world be known

All leisure hours while miss at home sojournd
Past in preparing till new routs returnd
Or tittle tattling oer her shrewd remarks
Of ladys dresses or attentive sparks
How Mr So and so at such a rout
Fixd his eyes on her all the night about
While the good lady seated by his side
200   Behind her hand her blushes forced to hide
Till consious Miss in pity she woud say
For the poor lady turnd her face away
And young Squire Dandy just returnd from france
How he first chose her from the rest to dance
And at the play how such a gent resignd
His seat to her and placed himself behind
How this squire bowd polite at her approach
And Lords een nodded as she passd their coach
Thus miss in raptures woud such things recall
210   And Pa and Ma in raptures heard it all
But when an equal woud his praise declare
And told young madam that her face was fair
She might believe the fellows truth the while
And just in sport might condescend to smile
But frownd his further teazing suit to shun
And deemd it rudeness in a farmers son
Thus she went on and visited and drest
And deemd things earnest that was spoke in jest
And dreamd at night oer prides uncheckd desires
220   Of nodding gentlemen and smiling squires
To Gretna green her visions often fled
And rattling coaches lumberd in her head
Till hopes grown weary with too long delay
Caught the green sickness and declined away
And beauty like a garment worse for wear
Fled her pale cheek and left it much too fair
Then she gave up sick visits balls and plays
Were whispers turnd to any thing but praise
All were thrown bye like an old fashiond song
230   Were she had playd show woman much too long
And condecended to be kind and plain
And 'mong her equals hoped to find a swain

Past follys now were hatful to review
And they were hated by her equals too
Notice from equals vain she tryd to court
Or if they noticed twas but just in sport
At last grown husband mad away she ran
Not with squire Dandy but the servant man

    Young farmer Bigg of this same flimsey class
Wise among fools and with the wise an ass   240
A farming sprout with more then farmers pride
Struts like the squire and dresses dignified
They call him rich at which his weakness aimd
But others view him as a fool misnamed
Yet dress and tattle ladys hearts can charm
And hes the choice with madams of the farm
Now with that lady strutting now with this
Braced up in stays as slim as sickly miss
Shining at christmass rout and vulgar ball
The favourite spark and rival of them all   250
And oft hell venture to bemean his pride
Tho bribes and mysterys do their best to hide
Teazing weak maidens with his pert deciet
Whose lives are humble but whose looks are sweet
Whose beauty happen to outrival those
With whom the dandy as an equal goes
Thus maids are ruind oft and mothers made
As if bewitchd without a fathers aid
Tho nodds and winks and whispers urge a guess
Weakness is bribed and hides its hearts distress   260
To live dishonourd and to dye unwed
For clowns grow jealous when theyre once misled
Thus pointed fingers brand the passing spark
And whispers often guess his deeds are dark
But friends deny and urge that doubts mislead
And prove the youth above so mean a deed
The town agrees and leaves his ways at will
A proud consieted meddling fellow still

    Nature in various moods pursues her plan

270   And moulds by turns the monkey or the man
With one she deals out wisdom as a curse
To follow fortune with an empty purse
The next in opposite extreams is bred
Oerflowing pockets and an empty head
Beggars in merit share a squires estate
And squires untitled meet a beggars fate
Fortunes great lottery owns nor rules nor laws
Fate holds her wealth and reason rarely draws
Blanks are her lot and merit vainly tryes
280   While heedless folly blunders on the prize

      Young Headlong Racket to the last akin
Who only deals more openly in sin
And apes forged love with less mysterious guile
A high flown dandy in its lowest stile
By fashion hated with the vulgar gay
And deems it wit to tempt their steps astray
No maid can pass him but his learing eye
Attempts to prove her forward or too shy
He brags oer wine of loves his wits has won
290   And loves betrayed – and deems it precious fun
Horses and dogs and women oer his wine
Is all his talk and he believes it fine
For virtue now is such a trifling name
That vice can prey ont unexposed to blame
And fools may join him but to common sense
His head pleads empty and has no pretence
He courts his maids and shuns the better sort
And hunts and courses as a change of sport
And hates all poachers game destroying brutes
300   Altho with both the name as aptly suits
With this one difference darkness brings their prey
And he more brazen murders his by day
And thus he lives a hated sort of life
Loves wedded wantons while he scorns a wife
Prepares by turns to hunt and wh—e and shoot
Less then a man and little more then brute

      Next on the parish list in paltry fame

Shines Dandy Flint Esqʳ whose dirty name
Has grown into a proverb for bad deeds
And he who reads it all thats filthy reads   310
Near did a single sentence more express
Of down right evil or of goodness less
Than Dandy Flint grown old in youthful shame
By loathed diseases which no words may name
And worn so spare that wit as passing bye
Swears Nick will thread him thro a bodkins eye
A sot who spouts short morals oer his gin
And when most drunk rails most against the sin
A dirty hog that on the puddles brink
Stirs up the mud and quarrels with the stink   320
Abusing others in his cants deciet
To come off victor when the rest are beat
His mask is but of lawn and every space
Lets in new light to show cants crimping face
He apes the lamb and is a wolf in grain
And guilty darkness dares the light in vain
Thus fools by making others failings known
Become the self accusers of their own
So Dandy Flint may rail it nothing weighs
Sense takes the slander of a fool for praise   330

    These are the things that oer inferiors flirt
That spring from pride like summer flyes from dirt
And teaze and buzz their summer season bye
Bantering the poor and struggling to be high
And shall such knaves 'neath flatterys garment hide
Or fear damp truth to turn its glass aside
The plea is urgd not but to common sense
Reason and truth will stand its own defence
Whilst dark hypocrisy affects the cheat
The real bitter mocks a seeming sweet   340
But whoso dealeth openly in shame
Must bear being noticed by his proper name
As he who thrusts his phiz in every glass
Meets a reflection be it man or ass
And can they thus who love themselves to view
Chuse to be vexd to find the picture true

Be as it will none but the base are bit
And satire shows them as they chuse to sit
Which if disliked they may improve with ease
350 And make the likeness [better] if they please
And satire stingless – follys and defects
While yet defective still its glass reflects
But when they cease to be as heretofore
It suits with others and is theirs no more

Some of the old school yet my verse coud tell
And one from boyhood I remember well
Who near aspired on follys wings to soar
A plain mean man scarce noticed from the poor
Who near expected as he walkd the street
360 Bows from inferiors whom he chancd to meet
Inferiors bred from fashions idle whim
Equals and neighbours all appeard to him
And tho wealth scornd in such low walks to go
And pride disdaind and called his manners low
He sought nor paid prides homage unto man
But lived unshining in his humble plan
And when his rights tyrannic power assaild
His courage triumphd tho his pocket failed
For he was doomd to feel that worldly curse
370 An upright spirit and an empty purse
Nor did he try the shamless fault to cure
Still keeping honest and remaining poor
But he has left and one of different race
Spoilt his old mansion and supplied his place
Nor left he there in seeking were to dwell
One heart save prides but inly wishd him well
Thus fortune oft dishousd by blinded guess
Bids honour starve and knavery meet success
Smiles on the wickeds ways their hopes to glad
380 And sinks the good man to maintain the bad

Proud Farmer Cheetum turnd a rogue by stealth
Whom prosperous times had ripend into wealth
Hunting and shooting had its ceasless charm
When his full purse cared little for a farm

A trusty hand was left to plough and plan
The double trade of master and of man
He kept his stud for hunts and races then
And dogs fed even better then his men
Bought loves and changed them when the freak was
    old
And drank his wine without a wife to scold   390
And gaind a dashing name and livd in style
And wore a mask to profit byt the while
For he who dares to do a deed of shame
Feels none and only knows it by the name
And made large credit while his name was good
For all woud trust him draw on whom he woud
A man so stylish none coud dream to doubt
Till changing times the secret brought about
The grains sunk price oer knaverys tricks was thrown
And others failings well excused his own   400
The times he said and frownd disturbd and sad
Needed no comment to explain them bad
So ere he broke he honestly confest
His wealth all gone and credit had the rest
And proved to all a smuggling rogue too late
Cheat creditors – turnd bankrupt – and still great
Hunts shoots and rackets as he did before
And still finds wealth for horses dogs and whore
And dogs and wh—— and horses in his train
Are all that have no reason to complain   410
These show his kindness in their varied ways
And gild his rotting name with dirty praise
Like as when brooks are dry the village sinks
Boast their full dingy tide that flows and stinks
That seems to boast when other streams are dry
'Neath summer suns how brave a dyke am I'

  Old Saveall next whose dirty deeds and fame
Might put a young bards silken lines to shame
But my plain homespun verse lets none escape
Nor passes folly in its rudest shape   420
When satires muse puts on a russet gown
Tho vermin start as game she runs them down

So Saveall shall have place whom fortunes smiles
Unmixed with frowns hath made him known for miles
Famous for riches and by knavery prized
And famed for meaness and by work despised
Who trys to buy a good name and decieve
With fair pretentions that but few believe
Who seldom swears and that but now and then
430   A smuggled oath when vexd by better men
That beard hypocrisy with honest grace
And tears the mask from cants decieving face
Yet in religion he is made elect
And buys with wine the favours of the sect
Making each spouter welcome when he comes
And turning beggars from their fallen crumbs
Pleading up charity in whining tones
And driving dogs at dinner from the bones
The scraps which beggars plead for serve his swine
440   So their lorn hopes seek other doors to dine
The broken bones enrich his land for grain
So dogs beneath his table wait in vain
On neighbourly good will he often dwells
And in dry times locks up his very wells
And if twas but of worth we might suppose
Hed even save the droppings of his nose
Such is this Saveall first of fortunes fellows
Famous for wealth great farms and small beer cellars
With the elect most saintish or most civil
450   And with the rest a cunning knave or devil

Poor honour now yields to the stronger side
A wrinkld maid turnd stale and past her pride
Knavery and cant in triumph take her place
Unblushing strumpets with a tempting face
Religion now is little more then cant
A cloak to hide what godliness may want
As painters deaths to make the terror less
Wrap their dry bones within a cheating dress
The world is of a piece words mostly make
460   The little difference for distinctions sake
Vice must own bad so virtue takes the best

Coarse is the one mere cobweb is the rest
And when encroaching vice with cunning deeds
To make a hole in virtues garb succeeds
Tis but indeed a customary case
She darns it up as none may spy the place
And if once caught by slanders jealous eye
Tho breaches double and holes multiply
Virtue awhile turns penitent and then
Like rifled maid her title claims agen   470
Their prayers are read as old accustomd things
And offerd up for all souls save the kings
They love mild sermons with few threats perplexd
And deem it sinful to forget the text
Then turn to business ere they leave the church
And linger oft to comment in the porch
Of fresh rates wanted from the needy poor
And list of taxes naild upon the door
Little religion in each bosom dwells
And that sleeps sound till sundays chiming bells   480
When from each shelf is regularly took
The weekly wanted pious dusty book
Seeking the church an hours good prayers they read
And hear a sermon as the all they need
Then read when home the reccolected text
And lay religion by till sunday next
Some with reform religions shade pursue
And vote the old church wrong to join the new
Casting away their former cold neglects
Paying religions once a week respects   490
They turn from regular old forms as bad
To pious maniacs regular[l]y mad
A chosen race so their consciet woud teach
Whom cant inspired to rave and not to preach
A set of upstarts late from darkness sprung
With this new light like mushrooms out of dung
Tho blind as owls i' th' sun they livd before
Consiet inspired and they are blind no more
The dru[n]ken cobler leaves his wicked life
Hastes to save others and neglects his wife   500
To mend mens souls he thinks himself designd

And leaves his shoes to the uncalld and blind
He then like old songs runs the scriptures oer
And makes discoverys never known before
Makes darkest points as plain as A B C
And wonders why his hearers will not see
Spouts facts on facts to prove that dark is light
And all are blind till he restore their sight
And swears the old church which he cast away
510 As full of errors and as blind as they
And offers prayers no doubt as prayers are cheap
For chosen shepherds to his worships sheep
Thinking the while if such the will of fate
Self might become a hopeful candidate
And doubtless longs shoud reformation call
To leave his own and take his neighbours stall
Part urgd as scripture more as self consiet
To suit his ends each passage he repeats
And in as various ways each fact he weaves
520 As gossips riddles upon winter eves
Now storming threats now pleading comforts mild
In puleing whine soft as a sucking child
The[y] cant and rave damnations threats by fits
Till some old farmer looses half his wits
Looks back on former sins tho loath to doubt
Groans oer a prayer and thinks himself devout
Then learnings lookd on as an idle jest
And the old cobler preaches far the best
Who smooths with honied hopes the deep dyd sinner
530 And earns reward – a lodging and a dinner
Their former teachers as blind guides they mock
Nor think them chosen for the crazy flock
The crazy flock believe and are depraved
And just in time turn ideots to be saved

The Ranter priests that take the street to teach
Swears god builds churches where so ere they preach
While on the other hand protestant people
Will have no church but such as wears a steeple
Thus creeds all differ yet each different sect

From the free agents to the grand elect   540
Who cull a remnant for the promised land
That wear heavens mark as sheep their owners brand
Each thinks his own as right and others wrong
And thus keeps up confusions babel song
While half the tribes at bottom are no more
Then saints skin deep and devils at the core
Who act by customs and as custom shows
Lay bye religion with their sunday cloaths
Religions aim is truth and different creeds
By different channels for that aim proceeds   550
But many wander muddy by the way
And dark with errors struggle far astray
Till weary with the toil they fainter creep
And then like stagnant waters stink and sleep
Religions truth a plain straight journey makes
Which falshoods wandering never overtakes
As gold when purified flows free from dross
And leaves the worthless mixture without loss
So from black errors truths eternal morn
Mounts into light and smiles the night to scorn   560
Tis not religion but its want when sects
Rail each at each to hide their own defects
For calmness quiet cheerfulness and love
Its essence is to aid our hopes above
Tis vain philosophy that would decieve
The[y] heer too much to doubt or to believe
What is and was we feel – what is to be
Truth nothing knows tis guess pretends to see
Een earths least mysterys are above our skill
And would-be-gods are but her childern still   570
Wisdom still searching with her flickering flame
Lost in her mysterys dwindles to a name
Whence goeth light when evening hides the sun
And whence the darkness when the night be done
Hither it cometh – aye – and there it goes
Is the whole sum which mighty wisdom knows
So resignation should the worst befall
And faith to hope the best is best of all

Old Ralph the veriest rake the town possesd
580 Felt sins prick deep and all his crimes confest
Groand oer confessions to his ranting priest
And prayd and sang and felt his soul released
The new births struggles made him wonderous wan
And feebly prayd at first the baby man
Twixt doubts and fears yet viewd the cured complaint
And scarce percieved the devil from the saint
But soon the 'outward man' grown godly mad
Felt the good spirit triumph oer the bad
And cants dull prayers too lame to visit heaven
590 Lookd oer past sins and fancied all forgiven
He then whind lectures in a happier strain
And coaxd poor sinners to be born again
Shund old companions once beloved so well
As condemnd transports on the way to hell
And prayd and sang from sin and pain releasd
And smoothd his hair and fashiond for a priest
Old women heard him with oerjoyd delight
Some cryd and sind and others turnd out right
Theyd read the gospel studied good St Paul
600 But ralp[h]s good doctrine was the best of all
From him they found their old religions stuff
Was nought but like a play at 'blind mans buff'
A pathless journey in a starless night
Till good St Ralp[h] restored the way to light
And thus as priest he exercised his wits
Forcd men to prayers and women into fits
And heard and cured each difficult complaint
And midst his flock seemd little less then saint
But hell untired with everlasting watch
610 (The fox grows cunning when preys hard to catch)
Crept into Ralphs new planted paradise
And met success in tempting him to vice
A simpering eve did in his garden dwell
And she was fair and he grew fond – and fell
Twas love at first but een when that began
The sinking saint grew more and more the man
And with his eve so treache[r]ously fair
Coud feel more joy then kneeling down to prayer

Yet still he prayd nor deemd his case so bad
As stone blind sinners tho his heart was sad   620
The bible still he read with saintly looks
And deemd all others as ungodly books
Unless a patch of scripture here and there
Redeemd each page and made them godly ware
Tho sinfull love had overpowerd his skill
With other sins he kept unspotted still
He drank nor swore and when a lye was told
Twas just gains trifle when he bought and sold
When bretheren met he woud his joys express
Groand while they prayd and said amen by guess   630
Then 'da— and blame ye' hed no further dare
Hell coud not urge the fallen man to sware
Till the compleation of his serpent sin
Urgd by the devil sunk him to the chin
Eve tho beguild forbidden fruit to taste
Had lovd an adam ere she loved the priest
And ere disgrace had ripend into light
Ralph had no power to wed her and be right
His fate was evident it came at last
His sheep was judge and shepherd ralph was cast   640
Then drink and rackett joind their former friends
And new born saint in the old sinner ends

    Next comes a name who spite of all controuls
Reigns oer the bodys ills as Ralph the souls
A mighty doctor – what so thickly sown
That een the Parish can a doctor own
Yes own one too whose power so splendid shines
As een to name illuminates my lines
For every mouth is puckered with his skill
So sing his patients and so say his bill   650
The worst disease he does so quick subdue
That makes some think the devil helps him through
But what care they who helps – if pain endured
So long before he rose can now be cured
By reading in their water all their ails
And conjuring medicines up that never fails
Thus all the country join his fame to raise

And few but Dr Urine gets the praise
So now for skill the parish rules the roast
660   Renowned for Quacks that Citys cannot boast
– Ah where in City or in Town can dwell
Famed Dr Urine thy rare parrarell
No where indeed to match at once with thee
Thy mighty fame and humble pedigree
But can that taint the Laurel on thy brows
'Cause thou wert wont to docter Swine and cows
And rose to fame as fame was took by force
From giving judgment on a cholicked horse
To read the water of poor sickly clowns
670   And ease them not of illness but their crowns
Tho every ill swims on thy majic glass
And at thy conjuring bidding rise and pass
Like Mackbeths murdered spirits grimly on
And thou thy powers scheme cures for every one
Een from the boasting of thy self – and thine
Thy duped deciples – such thy fame doth shine
As if the dead were not beyond thy skill
But might be quickened from thy power and pill –
The poor old woman now half blind and lame
680   With age – has room to curse thy greedy fame
For she herself had fame ere thou hadst thine
And did as doctress of the Village shine
Tho one rare salve was cure for every sore
That Salve and that famed Doctress' race is oer
Say Dr Urine why – (and dont deride
My gossiping enquirey) shouldst thou hide
In such poor paltry Parish this renown
As seems well worthy of the finest town
Nay rather City for Im sure thy name
690   And Waterbottles might extend thy fame
To every patient that had death to fear
Then say good Docter why so linger here
Thourt no great 'schollard' that the learned tell
And all that buy thy drugs might know as well
But it so turns and lucky for thy pelf
Thy patients are less 'schollards' then thyself
– But what of learning words mispelt is small

Drawbacks on knowledge that gives cures for all
Distempers and diseases as he wills
And almost cures a broken limb with pills   700
The learned faculty are tools to thee
And from thy powers like thy complaints will flee
Then why thus linger in the worst of towns
To cure and hear the praise of foolish Clowns
But fools perhaps may be thy only game
To feed thy pockets and encrease thy fame
If so think not in greater towns to shine
Where skill would bid thy juggling tricks decline
And bright eyed reason send thee hasty back
Proving thee what thou really art a quack   710
So Dr Urine in thy nest remain
And till the dull dark age of fools be past
As conjuror and Water Doctor reign
Then drop into thy grave – a Quack at last

   In politics and politicians lies
The modern farmer waxes wonderous wise
Opinionates with wisdom all compact
And een coud tell a nation how to act
Throws light on darkness with excessive skill
Knows who acts well and whos designs are ill   720
Proves half the members nought but briberys tools
And calls the past a dull dark age of fools
As wise as solomons they read the news
Not with their blind forefathers simple views
Who read of wars and wishd that wars woud cease
And blessd the king and wishd his country peace
Who markd the weight of each fat sheep and ox
The price of grain and rise and fall of stocks
Who thought it learning how to buy and sell
And he a wise man who coud manage well   730
No not with such old fashiond idle views
Do these news mongers trafic with the news
They read of politics and not of grain
And speechify and comment and explain
And know so much of parliment and state
Youd think them members when you heard them prate

And know so little of their farms the while
That can but urge a wiser man to smile

Young Brag a 'jack of all trades' save his own
740 From home is little as the farmer known
He talks with all the equal and the high
Equally ready to tell truth or lie
His betters view him in his just deserts
But equals deem him one of mighty parts
Opinions gratis gives in mens affairs
Fool in his own but wonderous wise in theirs
Upon his talents friends were strongly bent
Mistook his parts and off to school he went
A young aspiring hopeful youth at least
750 Whose parents deemd him fashiond for a priest
Twas somthing urgd the dissapointed view
With which religion had the least to do
Tho they baskd blessd in fortunes wealthy sun
They yearnd for more to bless their hopeful son
Whom school and colledge both had vainly taught
And learnd young hopeful to be fit for naught
His friends decievd beheld the faded charm
Resignd weak hopes and placed him in a farm
And there he lives and to great skill pretends
760 And reigns a god among his farming friends
Scrats paragraphs and sends them to the News
Signd 'constant reader' lest they shoud refuse
The illspelt trash on patriotic cavils
Leaving correction to the printers devils
Skits upon those by whom theyre never read
Who might as well write Letters to the dead
Or puffs upon himself in various ways
Whom none but self will either read or praise
And Poems too the polishd patriot chimes
770 Stanzas to Cobbets truth and Comic Ryhmes
To which he fits a hacknied tune that draws
From patriot dinners echoes of applause
And in the next weeks news out comes the treat
From 'constant reader' of the drunken feat
Were so much wine is lavishd in the strain

As even to make the reader drunk again
Were every dish on which the knaves regale
Find places there but common sense and ale
For common sense is grown too tame to teach
And ales too low to aid a patriots speech   780
And morts of speeches made to back reform
That raised applauses like a thunder storm
And almost loosd the rafters from their pegs
While chairs and tables scarce coud keep their legs
Reeling amid the hiccups and hurra's
And glass[es] rung and almost dancd applause
Nor will he pass his comic singing oer
For they too set the table in a roar
And then concludes it with the pompous clause
– Success to patriots and the good old cause   790
A hacknied tune which patriots daily sing
Like variations of 'God save the King'
But when election mobs for battle meet
And dirty flags and ribbons throng the street
Hunting for votes some little borough town
Tis there his genius meets the most renown
When on the hustings bawling spouters throng
Who fight and war like women with the tongue
All speakers and no hearers were the crys
Piles up confusions babel to the skys   800
And croaking at the top in proud renown
Each party sits till tother pulls him down
Here shines our orator in all his plumes
Nor prouder bantum to a dung hill comes
Then he to crow and peck and peck and crow
And hurl bad english at retorting foe
No hungry magpie round a rotten sheep
A longer song of nonsence up can keep
Were small words all their utmost powers engage
And monnysyllables swell mad with rage   810
Who martyrs like to freedoms noble cause
Are choaked by scores in hiccups and hurras
The rest awhile in thick disorder flye
And from his mouth like crackers bounce and dye
'I said' – 'says I' and – 'then' – 'he said' – 'says he'

Are the chain balls of his attillery
That storm and threaten at the deadly breach
And link the weapons of his broken speech
The head and tail piece setting off and close
820   That throws each sentence at his sneering foes
And when his monny syllables have spent
Their rage and given his utmost fury vent
And wore the cant thread bare that serves the throng
Like summers cuckoo tune for every song
Of 'Rotten boroughs' – 'bribery' – 'tyrants' – 'slaves'
Were selfs a patriot and opposers knaves
To fill the void his lack of words will cause
He bawls out freedom and expects applause
Then bows his head in oratorial grace
830   And exit makes to give new speakers place
So have I seen the schoolboy in his sport
(When playing soldiers) honours praise to court
Spout to his fancied army on parade
Bawling of valour ere the assault was made
Then drew his 'wooden sword' and led the way
To storm their castles and commence the fray
Pointing their pellets at unconsious foes
At bantum cocks that on the dung hill crows
When pop each gun went to commence the quarrel
840   Nor scared the flye that settled on the barrel
He ryhmes election squibs and meets applause
From party critics that support his cause
His fustian wit trots wild on broken feet
Jostling the readers patience from his seat
Half prose half verse they stagger as they go
And after fashions follys dribbling flow
One line starts smooth and then for room perplext
Elbow along and knock against the next
And half its neighbour then a stop marks time
850   To close the sense – what follows is for ryhme
Pert forwardness and insolent consiet
In bard and patrons close as circles meet
All that is bad from one to tother jumps
Both play at cards and turn up knaves as trumps
And his bad wares in credits way to push

He boasts theres nought to make the modest blush
Tho common sense he neither fears or heeds
Who finds a cause to blush at all she reads
To see its name with fools as partners shown
And cursed with trash which dullness shrinks to own   860
Yet in the columns of the weekly News
They shine as laureat odes to 'Pinks' or 'Blues'
Where humbug patron of cants tinsel gauds
Reads and with Fudge so sanctions and applauds
One blows the bubble up with puffing sides
And tother marks till stiff necked how it rides
Bawling aloud till hoarse 'look here now there'
Till mobs throng round to wonder and to stare
Then flattery puffs a critique in their cause
And gain throngs in with interest and applause   870
So boys with their tobacco pipes and suds
Play while one bubble after tother scuds
Look there a fine one goes and there another
How bubble two beats bubble one his brother
Then blows again with cheeks distended wide
Till like the frog he almost bursts with pride
Then out goes bubble three and instant out
From gaping mouths come the applauding shout
That makes his pride and happiness redouble
And soap baloons flye up in many a bubble   880
Humbug still hailing with excess of joy
Who condescends to feed both men and boy
With this small difference the boys sports are stinted
Tho humbug praises theres no puff to print it
He games and drinks and rackets up and down
A low livd mocker of high life in town
And sips his wine in fashionable pride
And thrusts in scorn the homely ale aside
His fathers riches bought such foolish airs
But wasting fortunes een must need repairs   890
As parching summer checks the runnels haste
The greatest wealth will lessen spent in waste
Tho credit proves him poor his stubborn pride
Oer acts his purse and struggles dignified
Yet stung with tidings that his consience vents

He rails at tythes and hopes for falling rents
Curses all taxes as tyrannic things
And hates the pride of government and kings
Forgetting self tho on the brink to fall
900 A shade of mightier consequence then all
Turnd radical in spirit and in purse
He prays reform and deems the laws a curse
Speaks treasonous things before his friends and cousins
And toasts reforming patriots by dozens
And aping wit with ignorant delight
A village politician turns out right
Burdett and Brougham his Bibles place supplys
And these he reads and studys and applys
But choaks their wit to pass his narrow brains
910 And steals the stingless carcass for his pains
Like to the Daw dressed in the Peacocks coat
He gives proud utterance to each stolen note
While laughter roars he seems on clouds to walk
For laughter is the chorus of small talk
Election hums and Placards on the throne
He mars the joke and makes the rest his own
Runs reason mad in his unreasoning matters
And twists and tears poor common sense to tatters
Yet while he mimics second hand and storms
920 And mocks each echo hooting for reforms
And rants with oratorial pause and start
Each stale grown speech of patriots oer by heart
He meets applause in every spouting fit
By those who take impertine[n]ce for wit
Friends gape and wonder while they hear him preach
And swear it Ciceronian every speech
But others view him in wits sneard remark
A toothless puppy that can only bark
He hails his countrys foes his only friends
930 D—ms peace and prays for war that never ends
Its ruins lookd on as the way to wealth
And grace for all meals is reforms good health
And why is all this hubbub for reforms
This anxious looking for expected storms
That turns each fireside into parliments

In strong debates of taxes tithes and rents
Is aught of general good or general views
Sketchd in the pathway which reform pursues
Or is the rich mans lands or misers pelf
But grudgd in others to be claimd by self   940
Doubtless the reasons far more plain then good
Is far more true as such then understood
Our village politician clings no doubt
To one sole cause that moves the rest about
His general good perhaps is small akin
To self a core that smuggles in that skin
Taxes no doubt might be at peace and stand
If theyd sink claims on his conserns and land
And such forcd things as Landlords yearly claims
He hates no doubt – tho fear but inly blames   950
And views reform in but a selfish light
To make a level far as self is right
Turn Lords to farms or farmers change to Lords
Is the dear wish that with his heart accords
Or when all laws are ruind with the throne
Just but to make the farm he rents his own
Thus far no farther tho with reasons leave
Want pleads for times of adam and of eve
This must not be they toild for bread before
And some must still be rich and some be poor   960
To sink the many and exalt the few
Is still his creed in an extended view
Reform thus leveld to brags selfish will
Want still might toil and be contented still
With other nations mid tyranic strife
This miscalld mania[c] struggles oft to life
Fair is the mask that hides its visage first
But soon the infant to a fiend is nursd
That like a wolf howls hungerly and high
A cry for blood – and freedom apes that cry   970
For Freedom unrestraind forsakes her cause
And lawless pleasures are her only laws
Like as high tempests reckless whom they harm
Come headlong on their pleasures to perform
Too late the trees beneath their burthen groan

The lawless storm feels treason in that tone
And down its whole artillery lightning hail
And thunder comes the rebels to assail
Prostrate at once the groves in ruins lye
980   Their torn roots pleading pity from the sky
So with the tyrant whom he wills he blames
Mere treason is what ere his vengance names
And where that falls – defence – complaints – aye sighs
Are discontents and treasons in disguise
Thus laws grow lawless and the patriot dies
Dies and above his poor insulted dust
Fears made to sanction that the deed was just
Such is the case when freedom like a flood
Bursts out in mischief what was meant as good
990   So thy proud lilys haughty france was torn
Whose whitness dared the insulted light to scorn
And scorn did come and thou wert weak indeed
Torn down and trampled like the meanest weed
Thy laws a tyrants scoffing stock became
And thy white Flag blushed red for very shame
When by a tyrants pompous threats unfurled
To show its former weakness to the world
Who mocking liberty where none remained
With stronger fetters former rights enchained
1000   Heaven shield thee England in thy ancient cause
From tyrant governments and broken laws
Since freedom came and crowned thee free none dare
As yet to rouse thy Lion from its lare
Threats have assailed thee but as like the wind
They roared and into nothing rage resigned
And they may roar and bluster but in vain
So barks the Mastiff at his clanking chain
Nations in bonds can never cope with thee
For they alone are mighty who are free
1010   And mayst thou ever be the same as now
With victorys laurels blooming on thy brow
That scource from which thy every glory springs
A land of liberty as well as kings
Thus village politics – and hopes for pelf
Live in one word and centre all in 'self'

Thus village politicians urge repairs
And deem all governments as wrong but theirs
Cants juggling wisdom spurning reasons rules
The reasoning jargon of unreasoning fools
Versd in low cunning which to handle brief   1020
Is but a genteel title for a thief
Nay start not reader such harsh words to hear
Nor deem the pen of Satire too severe
What is that shuffling shadow of a man
Were selfs deceptions shine in every plan
Who spouts of freedom as the thing he craves
And treats the poor oer whom he rules as slaves
Who votes equallity that all may share
And stints the pauper of his parish fare
Who damns all taxes both of church and state   1030
And on the parish lays a double rate
Such is our heroe in his tyrant pride
Then is his honours title misapplied
Such with one breath scoff at the poors distress
And bawl out freedom for their own redress
True Patriotism is a thing divine
And far above a theme so mean as mine
To higher powers due praises may belong
But patriotism is above my song
Not that which tells its emptiness aloud   1040
Like quacks and pedlars to a gaping crowd
That pleads foul robbery in an honest stile
And feeds poor hope on honied words the while
That deems it honour urgd in knaverys cause
And highest merit to evade the laws
With words of peace and plenty thickly sown
Deceptions aimd at ignorance alone
Empty as frothing bubbles on the stream
Or shadowy banquets in a beggars dream
Ruins the mark the motly monster bears   1050
And vile hypocrisy the mask it wears
Cant as high priest around its alter prays
And preaches loud its mockery of praise
Oer blinded minds its poison quickly runs
But shrinks in mist from reasons searching suns

To those gilt Dagons knaves and fools may raise
Deceptions alters of decieving praise
And paint their claims as interest wills to paint
Call each a god a devil or a saint
1060 Truth will his godships mighty claims betray
And prove like Daniel that hes made of clay
These soft politic saints may freedom preach
And vacant minds believe the lies they teach
Who think them walking canaans flowing oer
With milk and honey for the starving poor
And sure enough their wants may richly fare
If like camelions they can feed on air
Their promises sown thick degenerate run
And mildew into broken ones when done
1070 And tho a plentious seed time dreams of gains
A blighted harvest falsifys the pains
Such promises to day to morrow straight
Like an old almanack is out of date
And they who break them no more credit breaks
Then Moors new year does for the olds mistakes
Thus freedom preaching is but knaverys game
And old self interest by a different name

But they alone are worthy of its claims
Who midst the storm that sanctions or defames
1080 Firm like the Oak on their first ground sojourn
Neath suns and winds that shines and shocks in turn
Who fear no scoffs nor hunt the cloak of bribes
Those smiling tempters of declaiming scribes
Meteors that dazzle with a vapours flame
That rise in gilded praise and set in shame
Tho barren vineyards patriots labour in
Their countrys good is all they strive to win
Tho rough the road they struggle to the last
And look with joy upon the journey past
1090 Their very faults are blessings misapplied
'And een their failings lean to virtues side'
Tho crowds be found to scorn and few to raise
The 'still small' anthem of deserving praise
Yet consience triumphs like a setting sun
And self illumined feels its best was done

For men like these the heathens praise did claim
Seats with the Gods and gave their deeds the name
And still for such fame pulls from freedoms tree
A bough that blossoms with posterity
And twines like Ivy gathering strength with time   1100
Green round the ruins of their native clime

    And such art thou – but why shoud I proclaim
Thy worth that hideth from the gaze of fame
And in the conscience of a noble cause
Shrinks like a hermit from the worlds applause
Yet worth like thine a share of fame shall meet
That falls like sunshine on thy calm retreat
That fame that found the Roman at his plough
Follows thy footsteps and applauds thee now
And little need hath verse of mine to tell   1110
Of one respected and beloved so well
And lest my humble muse unused to shine
Shoud with presumptive theme dishonour thee
I'll leave thy name to wortheir songs then mine
And pledge this offering to thy memory
Titles and power and riches and estate
All at thy birth conspired to make thee great
But these are baubles which distinction breeds
And are as shadows to thy noble deeds
Pomp is an insect that but makes display   1120
For one poor season and so fades away
Tho flattery fawns by wealth and titles moved
True worth alone can make the man beloved
And worth is thine that through thy life hath won
The praise of many and the scorn of none
For foes grow silent when they hear thy name
And sanction praises were they cannot blame
For thy whole life hath sought one common end
The slave to free the feeble to befriend
No pompous speechs which ambition vents   1130
Made thy name popular in parliments
No court intrigues a fawning hope to raise
Gilt thy first entrance with newspaper praise –
Mans general welfare and thy countrys good
Deeds on which honours noblest base hath stood

Were the first struggles of thy patriot skill
And wears through life thy whole ambition still
Labouring along in each unshining part
With simple truth and such an upright heart
1140 That when the poor hear thee their rights defend
They feel thee more their brother then their friend
And in such hearts thy name so good and just
Shall live behind and 'blossom in the dust'
And may thy names successors ever be
Branches proved worthy of their parent tree
To bloom unblighted on a glorious race
Shineing unsullied on the page of fame
And like the sunrise on an ancient place
Gild the past memory of thy worthy name
1150 Names without worth may be by beggars bought
Shadows of nothings that are less then naught
These will grow old like garments time will tear
Poor honours tinsel and make worse for wear
The proudest trials to prolong their date
When scut[c]heond pride turns rags and mocks in state
Aye marble bye and bye with sculpture deckt
Shall mingle with the ashes they protect
Brass eat its self away in fretting rust
And names on adamant shall fret to dust
1160 Worth and worth only has the longest run
And virtue graves it on the golden sun
Eternitys escutcheon there it shines
With every day renewed which nothing lines
Piering its influence on the happy day
While bad ones moulder in the night away
What is mere honour that so charms the sight
A bauble gilt a shadow cloathed in light
A pompous nothing pride extolleth high
A boast of blood that runs its channels dry
1170 To stagnate upon common shores at last
Honour in state what is the Farce when past
A veil death sends exposing tyrant knaves
To eke the refuse of ignoble graves
Honour in war the cannon vaunts so loud
What but poor insect weaving its own shroud

A danger where the bravest dare and die
For the cold praise that marble tombs supply
And such is honours all in every game
Like faithless friend she soon forgets their fame
And as a laccquey unto shame will turn   1180
With littleness and meaness to sojourn
So what was Pompeys Cesars in the past
Race horses dogs and coaches heir at last

   Mere titles without worth are withered bays
And paper crowns that mock at honours rays
The meanest tradesman in his flash attire
Struts from behind his counter an Esqr
Een knighthood from its throne is hurled afar
And fortune caught for clowns the fallen star
What honour wore times past Sir Ralph wears now   1190
Whose feats of prowess sprung from flail and plough
Whose grandame spun and darned the cloaths she wore
And rob[b]ed the dung hill to increase her store
Thus sprang the means that feed his present fame
And silver stars gild oer his little name
And just as much of honours light they leave
As pewter crests upon a paupers sleeve
The little odds thats hardly worth the name
Lie in the metal for the mans the same
While a good name however poor or small   1200
Grows great in value and outshines them all

   A shadow man between the two extreams
Of fat and lean like pharoahs hungry dreams
With visage such as frighted childern dread
When gossip stories haunt their dreams abed
In heart and head vain ignorant and dull
And fierce in visage as a baited bull
Appears the village constable who bears
The affairs of state and keeps them in repairs
Foremost in meetings he resumes his place   1210
And gives opinions upon every case
Reigning and ruling in the mighty state
A jackall makeshift for a majistrate

Keeping the tools of terror for each cause
When the starved poor oerstep his pigmy laws
To mark the paupers goods the parish brand
Is in his mansion ready at command
Titles around his name their honours bring
Like rags and tatters round the 'beggars king'

1220   Churchwardens Constables and Overseers
Makes up the round of Commons and of Peers
With learning just enough to sign a name
And skill sufficient parish rates to frame
And cunning deep enough the poor to cheat
This learned body for debatings meet
Tho many heads the parliment prepare
And each one claims some wisdom for its share
Like midnight with her vapours tis so small
They make but darkness visible withall
1230   Their secretary is the Parish Clerk
Whom like a shepherds dog they keep to bark
And gather rates and when the next are due
To cry them oer at church time from his pew
He as their 'Jack of all trades' steady shines
Thro thick and thin to sanction their designs
Who apes the part of King and Magistrate
And acts grand segnior of this turkish state
Who votes new laws to those already made
And acts by force when one is disobeyd
1240   Having no credit which he fears to loose
He does what ever dirty jobs they chuse
Knight of the black staff master of the stocks
And hand cuff keeper – tools that sadly mock
His dignity – for common sense will sneer
And half acknowledge in his passing ear
That such like tools and titles near was known
To grace a name so aptly as his own
For though with natural cunning fortified
His deeds will often grow too large to hide
1250   Tho' like a smugglers dealings shunning light
They peep thro' rents and often sprout in sight
Thus summons oft are served in hopes of pelf

To overcharge and get a fee for self
And village dances watched at midnight hours
In the mock errand of his ruleing powers
With feigned pretence good order to preserve
Only to break it if a chance shoud serve
For married clowns his actions closely mark
And jealous grow at whispers in the dark
Whence broils ensue – then from the noisey fray   1260
Himself hath made sneaks unpercieved away
Like to the fox whom yard dogs barks affright
When on the point of robbing roosts at night
Such is this Sancho of the magistrates
And such are most knaves of those petty states
Where cunning fools are only reckoned wise
Who best can hide their faults from others eyes
And bold assurance forging merits place
Takes credit to be bad were all are base
Whose Staff becomes his law and succour too   1270
The stoutest village rabble to subdue
Soon as he holds it in his mighty hand
It grows as potent as a magic wand
Clowns look and grow submissive at the view
As if the mighty weapon froze them thro
For when a Hudibrass oersteps the laws
A Ralph is ready to defend his cause
Tasking the pauper [his] labours to stand
Or clapping on his goods the Parish Brand
Lest he shoud sell them for the want of bread   1280
On parish bounty rather pind then fed
Or carrying the parish book from door to door
Claiming fresh taxes from the needy poor
And if ones hunger overcomes his hate
And buys a loaf with what shoud pay the rate
He instant sets his tyrant laws to work
In heart and deed the essence of a turk
Brings summons for an eighteen penny rate
And gains the praises of the parish state
Or seizes goods and from the burthend clown   1290
Extorts for extra trouble half a Crown
Himself a beggar that may shortly take

A weekly pittance from the rates they make
But the old proverb suits the subject well
Mount such on horseback and theyll ride to hell
Such is this fussy cur that well deserves
The business of the master whom he serves
The vilest thing neer crawled without its brother
And theyre as like as one Ass gets another
1300 One sets no job but tother barks to do't
Both for self interest lick the foulest foot
And spite of all the meaness and the stink
Picks up gains crumbles from the dirtiest sink
One name serves both and that I need not name
For all may by the color know the game
As hungry dogs know carrion by the smell
So all may know them by their ways as well
Coarse as such images but nought would do
But coarsest stuff to make the picture true
1310 As when some muse weeps over Tyburn tree
Hard words and hanging make the melody
So as they reign here let them hang together
Stinking when met like sinks in stormy weather
Tho natures marks are deep that all may scan
A knaves delusions from an honest man
Oppression often mourns the vile abuse
And flyes to justice – deemd of little use
Truth that coud once its own redresses seek
Is now deemd nothing and forbid to speak
1320 Driven like an exild king from past renown
Power took its place and keeps it with a frown
But tis well known that justice winks at crimes
A saying thats in season at all times
Or why should the poor sinning starving clown
Meet jail and hanging for a stolen crown
While wealthy thieves with knaverys bribes endued
Plunder their millions and are not pursued
Nay at the foot of Tyburns noted tree
They do deserving deeds and still go free
1330 Where others suffer for some pigmy cause
They all but murder and escape the laws
Skulking awhile in briberys dirty den

Then start new gilt and pass as honest men
And why shoud power or pride betray its trust
Is it too old a fashion to be just
Or does self interest inclinations bend
Aye Aye the Farmer is his worships friend
As parish priest from him he meets his tythes
Punctual as harvest wakes the tinkling sythes
Tho often grudgd yet he their hopes to glad   1340
Prays better harvests when the last was bad
And as he deals so honestly with him
It must be malice in the poor or whim
Who seek relief and lay on them the blame
And hopless seek it and return the same
Within the church where they on sabbath days
Mock god with all the outward show of praise
Making his house a pharisees at best
Gods for one day and Satans all the rest
The parson oft scarce puts his sermon bye   1350
Ere neath his pulpit and with mighty cry
The clerk anounces – what? – commandments meet
No – when these parish vestrys next shall meet
To fleece the poor and rob with vile command
Want of its bread too feeble to withstand
Altho its aching heart too often knows
Knaves call it debtor where it nothing owes
For in these Vestrys cunning deep as night
Plans deeds that would be treason to the light
And tho so honest in its own disguise   1360
Twould be plain theft exposed to reasons eyes
For the whole set just as they please can plan
And what one says all sanction to a man
Self interest rules each vestry they may call
And what one sticks for is the gain of all
The set – thus knavery like contagion runs
And thus the fathers card becomes the sons
Both play one game to cheat us in the lump
And the sons turn up shows the fathers trump

    Here shines the man of morals Farmer Finch   1370
Smooth tongued and fine an angel every inch

In outward guise and never known as yet
To run in Taverns Brothels or in debt
In public life all punctual honest true
And flattery gives his graces double due
For pitys gifts are never public made
But there his name and guinea is displayed
In double views to answer prides desire
To purchase praise and to be dubbed Esquire
1380   A sunday never comes or foul or fair
That misses him at church throughout the year
The priest himself boasts as the mans reward
That he near preached a sermon but he heard
Such is the man in public all agree
That saints themselves no better men could be
But now of private life lets take the view
– In that same church and in that very pew
Where he each sabbath sings and reads and prays
He joins the vestry upon common days
1390   Cheating the poor with leveys doubly laid
On their small means that wealth may be defrayed
To save his own and others his compeers
He wrongs the poor whom he has wrongd for years
Making the house of prayer the house of sin
And placing Satan as high priest within
Such is this good church going morral man
This man of morrals on deseptions plan
So knaves by cant steer free from sins complaints
And flatterys cunning coins them into saints

1400   Tho justice Terror who the peace preserves
Meets more of slander then his deeds deserves
A blunt opinionated odd rude man
Severe and selfish in his every plan
Or right or wrong his overreasoning heart
Believes and often overacts his part
Tho pleading want oft meets with harsh replies
And truths too often listend too as lies
Altho he reigns with much caprice and whim
The poor can name worse governers then him

His gifts at Christmass time are yearly given   1410
No doubt as toll fees on the road to heaven
Tho charity or looses byt or wins
Tis said to hide a multitude of sins
And wether wealth-bought-hopes shall fail or speed
The poor are blest and goodness marks the deed
Tho rather leaning to the stronger side
He preaches often on the sins of pride
And oft while urging on the crimes of dress
His looks will tell the jealous were to guess
Vain offering mercys plea in hopes to cure   1420
How wasted pride might feed the wanting poor
And wether just or not his own whole plan
Sets the example as a plain drest man
His three cockt hat and suit in colour met
Were youths first fashion and he sticks it yet
The same spruce figure traced in memorys back
Een strangers know him as 'the man in black'
While playing boys on sundays without guess
Will scent their foe a furlong by his dress
Tho to complaints his aid is oft denyd   1430
Tho said too oft to shun the weaker side
Yet when foul wrongs are utterd in his ear
Farmers themselves meet reprimands severe
Poor trembling maids too learn his looks to dread
By sad forcd errands to his mansion led
His worships lectures are so long and keen
Theyre dreaded now as pennance once has been
Tho it is said what will not rumour say
There een was seasons when the priest was gay
That now and then in manhoods lusty morn   1440
His maids turnd mothers and were never sworn
Yet still he reigns what ever faults they find
A blunt odd rude good picture of his kind
Who preaches partial for both church and king
And runs reform down as a dangerous thing
And oft like hells its mystic deeds unravels
And dreads its name as childern dread the d——ls
Yet mixes often in election dinners
And takes his seat 'with publicans and sinners'

1450　Drinks healths and argues wether wrong or right
　　　　Nor ever flinches to be deemd polite
　　　　But healths gave out by young reforming sparks
　　　　He drinks in silence and disdains remarks
　　　　Or puts the profferd wine untasted bye
　　　　And waits some wiser speech to make reply
　　　　Anothers faults with him are quickly known
　　　　Yet needs a micriscope to find his own
　　　　He deems all wrong but him unless they be
　　　　Of the same cloth and think the same as he
1460　Thus self triumphant both in light and dark
　　　　He oft leaves reason and oer shoots the mark
　　　　And while he deems reform a knave and cheet
　　　　Extreams in both as equals nearly meet
　　　　For he who gains on reasons race the start
　　　　And good or bad thus overacts his part
　　　　Is quite as radical in reasons cause
　　　　As he who trys to trample oer the laws
　　　　What ever cause he banters or defends
　　　　Enthuseism baffles not befriends
1470　The wild mad clamours that its votarys raise
　　　　Urge those to ridicule who meant to praise
　　　　And hurts religion tho it wears a gown
　　　　As bad as deists who woud pull it down
　　　　And thus his reverence often sinks in faults
　　　　And dashes on and never own[s] nor halts
　　　　Ranters and Methodists his open foes
　　　　In person and in sermons hell oppose
　　　　With superstition hell brook no pretense
　　　　And deems them catholics in all but sense
1480　They in their turn oppose the urgd remark
　　　　And deem his worship grovling in the dark
　　　　Sifts the opinions which he puts in force
　　　　And strives to wreck him with his own discourse
　　　　Deeming the plan to which his pride doth cling
　　　　'That little learning is a dangerous thing'
　　　　From whence reformd opinionists proceed
　　　　That near had been had they not learnd to read
　　　　They prove such plans in arguments at length
　　　　A very pope in every thing but strength

And tho the cobler priest lacks no consiet 1490
His worship tires him and will not be beat
When the old snob despairing not resignd
Sighs while he sneers and pitys one so blind
Still with each rude assault he preseveres
Nor heeds the Coblers cant nor cares nor fears
And now and then his sermons length prolongs
To guard his flock against decietful tongues
And takes much trouble on a sabbath day
To lecture drunkards and drive boys from play
And tho from year to year unknown to use 1500
To keep his peace and sunday from abuse
Beside the circling cross upon the hill
The dancing Stocks maintain their station still
And as derision and decaying time
Weaken their triumph oer abuse and crime
The priest still mindfull of his ruling cares
Renews their reign in threatning repairs
Laws or religion or be what they will
Self will not yield but stickles to it still
And still he rules in every baffling plan 1510
The same head strong opinionated man

  But now grown old in reading sundays prayers
And keeping village morals in repairs
Till een his very spectacles refuse
To see the largest print that age can chuse
He seeks a curate to supply his place
A kinsman of his worships sacred race
Who ages back sought priesthoods place to teach
The only spot were bankrupts cannot reach
And meeting riches in prosperity 1520
Still chuse a scion from the family
To graft upon religions fruitful stock
Were blights near come ambitions hopes to mock
That bends with fruit when ere they like to pull
And bears all seasons and is ever full
So this young kinsman of his worships troop
That like to Levi keeps the charter up
Now fills with mighty lungs the plenteous place

Whose love of gain makes up for want of grace
1530 Who wears his priesthood with a traders skill
And makes religion learn to make her bill
Who ere he cures his sheep of their disease
Like lawyers studys oer the churches fees
Who ekes new claims on customs ancient price
When reason ruled and priests were not so nice
And sets on registers his raising mark
That used to fetch their sixpence to the clerk
And from the age enquiring staring clown
Extorts the monstrous charge of half a crown
1540 And if a wanderer leaves his wants to roam
And dies on other ills he meets from home
His church yard common for a bed is lost
And forfeits must be paid by double cost
And his jack all the clerk in double sense
Who sings his sunday task and counts his pence
Hies to his post instructed in his trade
To claim the fees before the grave is made
And marriage pays its earnest for a bride
Offering her fees before the knott is tyd
1550 And new made mothers that with thanks repairs
Seek gods kind love but pays the priest for prayers
With him self interest has a face of brass
A shameless tyrant that no claims surpass
Who shrinks at nothing and woud not disdain
To take a farthing in the ways of gain
Or less what ere his claims and fees enjoin
If such a fraction was a current coin
Such is the substitute put on to keep
The close shorn remnant of his worships sheep
1560 And bye and bye hopes at his friends decay
To be sole shepherd and recieve full pay
And is religion grown so commonplace
To place self interest foremost in the race
And leave poor souls in Satans claws confind
Crawling like crabs a careless pace behind
Excuse the priest he's prest with weighty cares
And tho the pauper dyes without his prayers
What if such worthless sheep slip into hell

For want of prayers before the passing bell
The priest was absent twas a daily song   1570
Yet none except the vulgar thought it wrong
Perhaps when death beds might his aid desire
His horse was sick and might a drink require
Or friends for just nessesitys might claim
His shooting skill to track the fields for game
And when they needed patridges or hares
The parish pauper coud not look for prayers
Or if he did indulge the foolish whim
What cared the priest – dye and be d—d for him
And he had land to shepherd where the wheat   1580
In a sly way the churches profit beat
Tho he kept one to manage of his kin
Yet self was foreman when the gain dropt in

   And dwells no memorys in the days gone bye
No names whose loss is worth a present sigh
Yes – there was one who priesthoods trade profest
'One whom the wretched and the poor knew best'
And in yon house that neighbours near the show
Of parish huts a mellancholy row
That like to them a stubble covering wears   1590
Decayd the same and needing like repairs
Superior only was the mansion known
Instead of mud by having walls of stone
There lived the Vicar once in days gone bye
When pride and fashion did not rank so high
Ere poor religion threw her weeds away
To mix in circles of the worldly gay
Ere hunting Parsons in the chace begun
And added salarys kept their dog and gun
To claim and trespass upon ground not theirs   1600
The game for shooting well as tythe for prayers
Ere sheep was driven from the shepherds door
And pleasure swallowed what might feed the poor
In that same time whose loss was keenly felt
The good old Vicar in this mansion dwelt
Plain as the flock dependant on his cares
Their week day comforts and their sunday prayers

Hed no spare wealth to follow fashions whim
And if he had she'd little joys for him
1610 He kept no horse the hunting sports to share
He fed no dogs to run the harmless hare
Hed nought to waste while hunger sought his shed
And while he had it they near wanted bread
His chiefest pleasure charity possest
In having means to make another blest
Little was his and little was required
Coud he do that twas all the wealth desired
Tho small the gift twas gave with greatest will
And blessings oer it made it greater still
1620 On wants sad tale he never closed his door
He gave them somthing and he wishd it more
To all alike compassions hand was dealt
And every gift tho small was deeply felt
The beggars heart dismantled of its fears
Leapd up and thankd him for his crust with tears
And ownd was worth rewarded as it ought
Hed claims to thousands were hed but a groat
Muttering their blessing as they turnd to part
Wishing his purse an equal to his heart
1630 Ah weres the heart so hardend at its core
Or eye so dead on what it pauses oer
That times sad changes fail to be severe
That sees his havoc and near drops a tear
The Vicars greensward pathways once his pride
His woodbine bowers that used his doors to hide
And he himself full often in his chair
Smoaking his pipe and conning sermons there
The yard and garden roods his only farms
And all his stock the hive bees yearly swarms
1640 Are swept away – their produce and their pride
Were doomed to perish when the owner dyd
Fresh faces came with little taste or care
And joyd to ruin what was his to rear
His garden plants and blossoms all are fled
And docks and nettles blossom in their stead
Before the door were pinks and roseys stood
The hissing goose protects her summer brood

And noisey hogs are free to wallow oer
What once was gravelld and kept clean before
The corner seat were weary hinds had rest   1650
The snug fire side that welcomd many a guest
Not fashions votarys these disdaind his door
But plain old farmers and the neighbouring poor
The one in harmless leisure to regale
To crack his wallnutts and to taste his ale
With miserys humble plea the other led
To tell his sorrows and to share his bread
These are decayed as comforts will decay
As winters sunshine or as flowers in may
These all are past as joys are born to pass   1660
Were lifes a shadow and were flesh is grass
Een memorys lingering features time shall rot
And this good man is nearly now forgot
Save on his tomb and some few hearts beside
Greyheaded now left childern when he dyd
Who from their parents all his goodness knew
And learnd to feel it as they older grew
When he was vanishd and the world was known
And troubles evil days became their own
Then woud they talk in sorrows gushing joys   1670
Of the good priest that preached when they were boys
And shake their heads and wish such godly men
And good old times woud come about agen
Full well may they regret the seasons gone
Such happy times that pride hath trampld on
Well may the past warm in the peasants praise
And dwell with memory as the golden days
When the old vicar with his village dwelt
Ere prides curst whimseys was so deeply felt
When farmers used their servants toils to share   1680
And went on foot to market and to fair
Not like the present petty ruling things
Disdaining ploughs from whence their living springs
And looking high among their betters now
Claim with the parson labours passing bow
Ere titled homage wore no vulgar names
Nor made a mockery to pretending claims

Yon cot when in its glory and its pride
Maintaind its priest and half the poor beside
1690 These were the times that plainess must regret
These were the times that labour feels as yet
Ere mockd improvments plans enclosed the moor
And farmers built a workhouse for the poor
And vainly feels them and as vainly mourns
As no hopes live betokening like returns
The cottage now with neither lawn or park
Instead of Vicar keeps the vicars clerk
Wolves may devour oppressions fiends may reign
Nones nigh to listen when the poor complain
1700 Too high religion looks her flocks to watch
Or stoop from pride to dwell in cots of thatch
Scenes too important constant business brings
That lends no time to look on humbler things
Too much of pleasure in her mansion dwells
To hear the troubles which the pauper tells
To turn a look on sorrows thorny ways
Like good samaritans of former days
To heal in mercy when foul wrongs pursue
And weep oer anguish as she once woud do
1710 Distress may languish and distress may dye
Theres none that hears can help them when they cry
Compassion cannot stoop nor pride alow
'To pass that way' with oil or honey now
Still there are some whose actions merit praise
The lingering breathings of departed days
Tho in this world of vainess thinly sown
Yet there are some whom fashion leaves alone
Who like their master plain and humble go
And strive to follow in his steps below
1720 Who in the Wilderness as beacons stand
To pilgrims journeying to the promised land
To give instructions to enquiring souls
And cheer the weak above the worlds controuls
To tend their charge and wanderers back restore
To rest the weary and relieve the poor

The past and present always disagree

The claims of ruin is what used to be
Old customs usuage daily disappears
And wash to nothing in the stream of years
The very church yard and its ramping grass   1730
And hollow trees remain not as it was
Far different scenes its nakedness displays
To those familiar with its guardians days
Tho holy ground and trees that round it grew
Ownd claims sufficient to be holy too
Religions humble plea was felt in vain
When ruin enterd with the hopes of gain
Its weak defence was trampled under foot
And all its pride laid level to its root
Its awthorn hedges surely sacred things   1740
That blushd in blossom to a many springs
Its hollow trees that time decayd in tears
And left to linger in the blight of years
Whose mossy finger scarrd on every grain
The trace of days that never come again
These old inhabitants are now no more
Oppression enterd and their reign was oer
Sure shades like these a natural end bespoke
Who'd thought their peace was ripening to be broke
Till other hearts the vicars place supplyd   1750
That preachd a life that practice oft belied
Then ancient tenants of a sacred spot
They fell like common trees and were forgot

   Ah sure it was a mellancholly day
That calld the good man from his charge away
Those poor lorn outcasts born to many cares
That shared his table welcome as his prayers
To them the bells worse tidings never gave
Then that which calld their guardian to the grave
To them no prayers so near their bosoms reachd   1760
As the sad lecture oer his coffin preachd
Theyd no more harvests now of hopes to reap
Een children wept to see their mothers weep
And pulld their gowns to ask and question when
Hed wake and come to give them pence agen

'Hell not sleep there for ever sure he wont
'Wholl feed and cloath us if the Vicar dont'
Thus lispd the babes and while their parents sighd
Muttering their blessings by the pasture side
1770   Warm repetitions of their griefs was given
And they hoped too to meet their friend in heaven

    Beside the charnell wall in humble guise
A small stone noteth were the vicar lyes
Were age slow journying on the sabbath day
Oft potters up to wipe the weeds away
And show enquiring youth with mournfull pride
That good mans name that once its wants supply'd
To hear it read and bring back days to view
And feel his goodness and his loss anew
1780   Blessing his name and praying as they weep
To be full soon companions of his sleep
To share with him the churchyards lonely peace
Were pride forgets its scorn and troubles cease
Were povertys sad reign of cares is oer
Nor tells its wants to be denyd no more
The last lorn hope and refuge that appears
Thro the dull gloom of lifes declining years

    Shoved as a nusiance from prides scornfull sight
In a cold corner stands in wofull plight
1790   The shatterd workhouse of the parish poor
And towards the north wind opes the creaking door
A makeshift shed for misery – no thought
Urgd plans for comfort when the work was wrought
No garden spot was left dull want to cheer
And make the calls for hunger less severe
With wholsome herbs that summers might supply
Twas not contrived for want to live but dye
A forced consern to satisfy the law
Built want this covering oer his bed of straw
1800   Een that cheap blessing thats so freely given
To all that liveth neath the face of heaven
The light of day is not alowd to win
A smiling passage to the glooms within

No window opens on the southern sky
A luxury deemd to prides disdainful eye
The scant dull light that forcefull need supplyd
Scorn frownd and placed them on the sunless side
Here dwell the wretched lost to hopeless strife
Reduced by want to skelletons in life
Despised by all een age grown bald and grey   1810
Meets scoffs from wanton childern in their play
Who laugh at misery by misfortune bred
And points scorns finger at the mouldering shed
The tottering tennant urges no replye
Turns his white head and chokes the passing sigh
And seeks his shed and hides his hearts despair
For pity lives not as a listner there
When no one hears or heeds he wakes to weep
On his straw bed as hunger breaks his sleep
And thinks oer all his troubles and distress   1820
With not one hope that life shall make them less
Save silent prayers that every woe may have
A speedy ransom in the peaceful grave
Close fisted justice tho his only friend
Doth but cold comforts to his miserys lend
For six days only it alows its fee
Pay scarce sufficient for the wants of three
And for the seventh which god sent to rest
The weary limbs of labouring man and beast
He too may pay for what blind justice cares   1830
Theyve nought for sunday but the parsons prayers

   He lived not from his cradle thus forlorn
Both friends and kindred blest his early morn
But kindred now are vanished all and gone
His friends turned foes and thus he lives alone
A Farm he rented in his prosperous days
And prides mouth never opened but to praise
Misfortune crossed his path he tried in vain
And sunk like Job but never rose again
His kindred pitied but no help supplied   1840
His friends were sought but friends their aid denied
Kin turned away and left his wants forlorn

And prides eye never heeded but to scorn
To him the whole wide world contained no friend
His griefs to sooth his weakness to defend
Look where he may all he possessed is fled
And he himself tho living seems as dead

 Old Farmer Thrifty reigns from year to year
 Their tyrant king yclypd an overseer
1850 A sad proud knave who bye a cunning plan
Blindfolds his faults and seems an honest man
He rarely barters when he buys or sells
But sets a price and there his honour dwells
He rails at cheating knaves for knaverys sake
And near asks double what he means to take
Shuns open ways which lesser rogues pursue
An outside christian but at heart a Jew
Each smooth deciet his blackend heart belies
And consience blushes thro the thin disguise
1860 He seems so honest so says Farmer Slye
That even childern may his bargains buy
And pays all debts too with a feignd good will
And rarely frowns to read a trades mans bill
While those deemd moderate charges rarely fail
To buy a welcome and to taste his ale
Upright and punctual every bargains made
A very quaker in affairs of trade
He preaches down the faults in neighbours known
Scorns other roguery just to hide his own
1870 Thus he mocks honour on deceptions creed
But let us read the riddle in the deed
Tho wealth nor makes nor want bemeans the man
With nought but luck the world and he began
Old men will tell you when the boy was small
How he blackd shoes and waited at the Hall
But natural cunning shone in early youth
And flatterys tongue which pride mistook for truth
Raisd by degrees the youngster into fame
And blotchd fates stigma from his little name
1880 Gilding like blemished fruit his failings oer
Thats fair without and rotten at the core

Thro all the names that wait on wealth and pride
From shoe black vile to valet dignified
He rose successively without a fall
And ownd the cunning power to please in all
And as the serpent yearly changed his skin
Some old face fled to take the youngster in
At length power blessd him with its highest stretch
Which good mens merits might despair to reach
No longer doomd in servitude to wait   1890
Next to the squire he managed his estate
Yclypd a Steward – strangers made their bow
And the squire took him as an equal now
While to neglect his former steward fell
For no one crime unless twas acting well
And soon the tyrant threw the mask aside
When wealth throngd in and power was gratified
Soon cloakd deciet that placed its owner there
To grasp at riches threw its visage bare
He raisd the rents of all the tennants round   1900
And then distrest them as in duty bound
And then askd leave of the contented squire
To rent the farm and had his hearts desire
The storm at first must burst upon the poor
That urgd wants curses as they passd his door
The humble hind that kept his cow before
And just kept want from creeping to his door
He viewd their comforts with a jealous heart
And raised their rents and bade their hopes depart
Yet loath to leave – their cows was sold for rent   1910
And the next year left nothing but complaint
Twas just as wished his plans was quickly known
Each spot was seized and added to his own
Others resignd and the half starving poor
Laid down their sufferings at their masters door
Unused to such complaints the easy squire
Was rousd to listen pity and enquire
The knave still ready up his sleeve to creep
Proved all as right and land as still too cheap
But friends familiar swore the squire was mad   1920
To think of reasoning with a man so bad

To see and suffer such uncloakd abuse
From one whose plans was shuffle and excuse
Such whispers urgd the easy Squire to shift
And Steward Thrifty then was turnd adrift
But not before his purse was filld with pelf
For knaves work quick and near loose sight of self
His nest was featherd ere his fame was old
And land was bought when farms was cheaply sold
1930 He now retires at ease and sells his grain
And strives to be an honest rogue in vain
With big round belly and sleek double chin
He reads the news and smokes and drinks his gin
And studys all the week oer gains affairs
And once a week at Chappel reads his prayers
And seems as striving former deeds to mend
Mild to a foe and coaxing to a friend
But to the poor his ways are still severe
Dwindled in Office to an overseer
1940 Still deaf to want that seeks him to be fed
He gives them curses in the lieu of bread
Or scoffing at their hopes tells them theyre free
To seek a law as tyranizd as he
Thus want still proves the stewards cankerd heart
And wealth beholds him ape 'the goodly part'
The one in nursing vengance while he starves
Is urged to curse him as he still deserves
The other blinded by his alterd plan
Forgives and takes him as a d—d good man
1950 Why art thou, beggars king wants overseer
To helpless poverty alone severe
On their dependance thou hast fatly fed
And can thy niggard hand deny them bread
He pleads bad times when justice chides his ways
Tho justice self is ill deserving praise
And is bad times the cause of such despair
Go ask the wretches who inhabit there
If past good times their hopes had ever blest
And left them thus so wretched and distrest
1960 Ask if their griefs can better times recall
Their startled tears tell plenty as they fall

And pitys heart can easy comprehend
That Farmer Thrifty never was their friend

Art thou a man thou tyrant oer distress
Doubtless thy pride woud scorn to think thee less
Then scorn a deed unworthy of that name
And live deserving of a better fame
Hurt not the poor whom fate forbad to shine
Whose lots were cast in meaner ways then thine
Infringe not on the comforts they posses   1970
Nor bid scant hope turn hopless in distress
Drive not poor freedom from its niggard soil
Its independance is their staff for toil
Take that away which as their right they call
And thourt a rogue that beggars them of all
They sink in sorrow as a race of slaves
And their last hope lives green upon their graves
Remember proud aspiring man of earth
Prides short distinction is of mortal birth
However high thy hated name may be   1980
Death in the dust shall humble pride and thee
That hand that formd thee and lent pride its day
Took equal means to fashion humbler clay
One power alike reigns as thy god and theirs
Who deaf to pride will listen humbler prayers
He as our father with the world began
And fashiond man in brotherhood with man
And learn thou this proud man tis natures creed
Or be thou humbled if thou wilt not heed
The kindred bond which our first father gave   1990
Proves man thy brother still and not thy slave
And pride may bluster in its little life
To tyranize with overpowering strife
Its turn shall come when proud insulting death
Shall bid it humble and demand its breath
And cannot these fierce tyrants of vain deeds
Dare in their pomp to intercept his speed
As well may rushes stiffen in the storm
And try to wear the oaks unyielding form

2000 As well may feathers float against the stream
      And shadows grow to substance in a dream
      Or clouds in tempests struggle to be still
      As pride to tamper and so baulk his will
      He meets them in their strength and torn from ease
      They groan and strive like tempests thro the trees
      While want from lifes dull shadows glad to run
      As pride went foremost and claimed all the sun
      Slips from the bitterness of mortal clay
      As calm as storms drop on an autumn day
2010 Death is the full stop that awaits to tell
      The period of our earthly chronicle
      The closing Finis that doth end the rude
      Essay of life and bids its tales conclude
      With all its failings in the lowly grave
      Existance ceases with the all it gave
      Wealth want joy anguish all do cease and lye
      More blank then shadows neath the smiling sky
      Leaving eternity to keep the key
      Till judgment sets all hopes and terrors free
2020 Pride and oppression here all meet their end
      And find their weakness when too late to mend
      With noiseless speed as swift as summer light
      Death slays and keeps his weapons out of sight
      Here thousands stript of earthly pomp and powers
      Met death and perished in unlooked for hours
      Their wealth availed not one in all the tribe
      Death hath no ears to listen to a bribe
      The rich fall poor into the grave and there
      The poor grow rich an equal claim to heir
2030 Deaths gloomy mansions owns no hall or throne
      But all lye equal – Death is lord alone
      Pomps trickerys in the grave are all forgot
      And worms and eyless skulls distinguish not
      The pomp that rotting in prides tomb doth lye
      From rubbish that fills up the slaves just bye
      Here tyrants that outbraved their God tho clay
      And for earths glory threw the heavens away
      Whose voice of power did like the thunder sere
      As anger hurried on the heels of fear

Ordaining hosts of murders at a breath 2040
How silent here doth sleep their rage in death
Their feet that trampled freedom to its grave
And felt the very earth they trod a slave
How quiet here they lye in deaths cold arms
Without the power to crush the feeble worms
Who spite of all the dreadful strife they made
Crept there to conquer and was not afraid
The warrior from wars havoc here detered
Bows before death lame as a broken sword
His power wastes all to nothingness away 2050
As showers at night wash out the steps of day

   Still lives unsung a race of petty knaves
Numerous as wasps to sting and torture slaves
The meanest of the mean a servile race
Who like their betters study to be base
Whose dung hill pride grows stiff in dirty state
And tho so little apes the little great
The Workhouse Keeper as old Thriftys man
Transacts the business on the tyrants plan
Supplys its tennants with their scanty food 2060
And tortures misery for a livlihood
Despised and hated by the slaves he wrongs
And een too low for satires scourging songs
So may they yet sink down more viler things
And starve as subjects were they reign as kings
Or when on earth their dirty triumph ends
May hells obscurity reward its frends

   A thing all consequence here takes the lead
Reigning knight errant oer this dirty breed
A Bailiff he and who so great to brag 2070
Of law and all its terrors as Bumtagg
Fawning a puppy at his masters side
And frowning like a wolf on all beside
Who fattens beef where sorrow worst appears
And feeds on sad misfortunes bitterest tears
Such is Bumtagg the bailiff to a hair
The worshipper and Demon of despair

Who waits and hopes and wishes for success
At every nod and signal of distress
2080 Happy at heart when storms begin to boil
To seek the shipwreck and to share the spoil
Brave is this Bumtagg match him if you can
For theres none like him living save his man
As every animal assists his kind
Just so are these in blood and business joined
Yet both in different colors hide their art
And each as suits his ends transacts his part
One keeps the heart bred villian full in sight
The other cants and acts the hypocrite
2090 Smoothing the deed where law sherks set the gin
Like a coy dog to draw misfortune in
But both will chuckl[e] oer their prisoner's sighs
And are as blest as spiders over flyes
Such is Bumtagg whose history I resign
As other knaves wait room to stink and shine
And as the meanest knave a dog can brag
Such is the lurcher that assists Bumtagg

Born with the changes time and chance doth bring
A shadow reigns yclypd a woodland king
2100 Enthrond mid thorns and briars a clownish wight
My Lords chief woodman in his titles hight
And base and low as is the vulgar knave
He in his turn for tyrant finds his slave
The bug-bear devil of the boys is he
Who once for swine pickt acorns neath the tree
And starving terror of the village brood
Who gleand their scraps of fuel from the wood
When parish charity was vainly tryed
Twas their last refuge – which is now denyd
2110 Small hurt was done by such intrusions there
Claiming the rotten as their harmless share
Which might be thought in reasons candid eye
As sent by providence for such supplye
But turks imperial of the woodland bough
Forbid their trespass in such trifles now
Threatning the dithering wretch that hence proceeds

With jail and whipping for his shamless deeds
Well pleased to bid their feeblest hopes decay
Driving them empty from the woods away
Cheating scant comfort of its pilferd blaze   2120
That doubtless warmd him in his beggars days
Thus knaves in office love to show their power
And unoffending helplessness devour
Sure on the weak to give their fury vent
Were theres no strength injustice to resent
As dogs let loose on harmless flocks at night
Such feel no mercy were they fear no bite

   Here comes one different to mere parish stuff
A host of talents met in Mr Puff
Knowing in all things ignorant of none   2130
To him mere genius is but farce and fun
While talent drops as from his finger ends
He knows all names – the greatest are his friends
And tho he never saw your face before
Hell jest at wit and run his nonsense oer
Familiar stuff so thick your shame assails
That even dogs to hear it wag their tails
He is so full of wisdom you would swear
Hed robbed the tree of knowledge till twas bare
And not contented with its store of fruits   2140
Had seized the trunk and grubbed it by the roots
And as for quoting Puffs the man to quote
As if hed read all that was ever wrote
Yet like his coat his taste must ape the fashion
So Shakspears pages are his greatest passion
Nor can a beggar even scrat his head
But theres what Shakspears on the matter said
To show by trifles how the fool has read
Are you a Bard – write prose too – very well
Puff deals in all and does in all excell   2150
And what he will not boast of having done
He casts that crumb of credit at his son
Mechanical pursuits to spout and write
'My son sir' rivals copper plate out right
Themes when a boy at school was never won

But foremost tho an infant stood 'My son'
And so between them knowledge is possest
Like Pharoahs kine they swallow all the rest
Sir Walter, Byron, as his friends he styles
2160 And at your ignorance thumbs his chain and smiles
Tho at the top of Fame[s] high towering tree
These share the worlds applause – poh so does he
If not in print he tells you bye and bye
He has a M.S. shall climb as high
Do you know half the Poets – thats as none
He strokes his chin and knows them every one
Poet Philosopher Mus[i]cian
In fact all fames are bound in his Edition
What ere is great Puff is – but nothing small
2170 All greatness dwells in Puff and Puff in all
If chance ere throws a Poet in his way
He worms him in their notice untill they
Half think theyve seen the smirking fiend before
With so much confidence he tongues them oer
But the mere Barber who is daily led
To clean his chin and drab his fustian head
If he but comes when he with friends hath got
He scorns the fellows speech and knows him not
Thus all small matters meet a rude rebuff
2180 From this self oracle renowned Hal Puff
And all thats great he treats as his compeers
A downright Ass in every thing but ears

    Others of this small fry as mean as base
May live unknown a pigmy reigning race
And sink to hell from whence their knavery came
As namless tribes unworthy of a name
Left on the dung hill were they reignd to rot
Hated while living and when dead forgot

    Here ends the Song – let jealousy condemn
2190 And deem reproofs they merit aimd at them
When pride is touchd and evil consience bit
Each random throw will seem a lucky hit
– If common sense its ears and eyes may trust

Each pictures faithful and each censure just
So let them rail – the proverbs truth is known
'Were the cap fits theyll wear it as their own'
Full many knaves sharp satires wounds have met
Who live in aqufortis dying yet
In burning Ink their scarecrow memorys dwell
Left to the torture of lifes earthly hell   2200
As markd and lasting as the thieves burnt brand
Who lives and dies with villian on his hand

Notes

l. 3 Clare is attacking the hypocrisy of much religion. The word 'saint' at this time was often used to refer to the fanatic adherents of dissenting sects.

l. 5 A useful account of the history of parochial administration in England is to be found in W. E. Tate's *The Parish Chest* (3rd edn, Cambridge, 1969).

In 1795 the magistrates of Speenhamland in Berkshire met to fix and enforce a living wage for farm labourers in view of the increasing price of bread. Instead they introduced the dole, whereby the difference between the wages a man earned and what it cost him to live – determined by the price of the loaf – should be met from parish rates. This system, where it was applied, meant that the farmer had little incentive to pay a living wage and the hard-working labourer suffered the indignity of being dependent on parish charity. In Clare's words 'Work for the little I choose to allow you and go to the parish for the rest – or starve'.

ll. 105–80 Many of the sentiments expressed here are re-echoed in Clare's prose passage 'The Farmer and the Vicar' (see 'John Clare' in the *Oxford Authors*, edited by Eric Robinson and David Powell (Oxford and New York, 1984), pp. 438–44).

ll. 113–14 An inevitable consequence of larger farms and more prosperous farmers was the gradual disappearance of the ancient tradition of labourers living under the same roof as their employers. Cobbett comments on this loss of intimacy between master and man, as does William Howitt in *The Rural Life of England* (London, 1838): 'At night the farmer takes his seat on the settle, under the old wide chimney – his wife has her work-table set near – the "wenches" darning their stockings, or making up a cap for Sunday, and the men sitting on the other side of the hearth, with their shoes off.'

l. 120 G. M. Trevelyan, *English Social History* (London, 1978), p. 416: 'Not only Cobbett but everyone else, complained that farmers were "aping their betters", abandoning old homely ways, eating off Wedgwood instead of pewter, educating their girls and dashing about in gigs or riding to hounds.'

l. 165 *the Speaker*: William Enfield's *The Speaker; or, Miscellaneous Pieces, Selected from the Best English Writers* (London, 1774) went into three more editions at least by 1790 and was a very popular anthology. Enfield, a Unitarian minister, had been a teacher at Warrington Academy and was a friend of Joseph Priestley.

l. 203 Demonstrates the eighteenth-century tradition of the Grand Tour. When peace came to Europe in 1815, the English discovered the Continent once again.

l. 221 *Gretna green*: the name of a village in Dumfriesshire just across the border, famous because runaway couples from England used to be married there according to Scots law, without the parental consent required in England for those who were under age.

l. 248 *Braced up in stays*: male corseting, the fashion of a conspicuous minority including the Prince Regent, became a subject of ridicule in the second decade of the nineteenth century, the age of the dandy.

l. 283 i.e. pretends to a love with a deceit he hardly bothers to hide.

ll. 315–16 i.e. according to a wit, Dandy Flint has become so thin that the Devil could push him through the eye of a needle.

l. 317 i.e. a drunkard who advocates scant morals over his gin.

l. 399 *The grains sunk price*: taking a base of 100 in 1790, corn prices stood at 187 in 1813, fell steeply after Waterloo and were as low as 113 in 1824. The small independent farmer suffered most as a result of the crash. Farmer Cheetum uses it as an excuse for his knavery.

ll. 436–46 An interesting comparison can be made with one of Clare's very early poems, previously unpublished, from Northampton MS 1, p. 6.

On Mr — locking up the Public Pump

> To lock up Water – must undoubted stand
> Among the Customs of a Christian Land
> An Action quite Uncommon and unknown
> Or only practic'd in this place alone
> A thing unheard of yet in Prose or Rhyme
> And only witness'd at this present time
> – But some there is – a stain to Christian Blood
> That cannot bear to do a Neighbour good
> – No! – to be kind and use another well
> With them's a torment ten times worse then hell
>
> Such Fiends as these whose charity wornt give
> The begging Wretch a single chance to live
> – Who to nor Cats nor Dogs one crumb bestows
> Who even grut[c]h the droppings of their Nose
> – Its my Opinion of such Marngrel curs
> Whom Nature scorns to own and Man abhors
> That could they find a f—t of any use
> They'd even burst before they'd set it loose!

l. 457 *painters deaths*: he may be referring to popular representations of the Dance of Death.

ll. 487–8 Clare writes in MS 14: 'I never did like the runnings and racings after novelty in any thing, keeping in mind the proverb "When the old ones gone there seldom comes a better". The "free will" of ranters, "new light of methodists", and "Election Lottery" of Calvanism I always heard with disgust and considered their enthusiastic ravings little more intelligable or sensible then the belowings of Bedlam'. See E. Robinson, *The Autobiographical Writings of John Clare*, pp. 25–6.

l. 535 *Ranter*: originally a member of a sect of seventeenth–century English antinomians, the word Ranter in the nineteenth century was applied colloquially to nonconformist (especially Primitive Methodist) preachers. For Clare's interest and involvement in Dissent see Mark Minor, 'John Clare and the Methodists: A Reconsideration', *Studies in Romanticism*, 19 (Spring 1980).

l. 594 *condemnd transports*: transportation to an overseas penal settlement had long been an accepted form of punishment.

ll. 643–714 Clare wrote two other satirical poems about avaricious doctors, both based on fact – 'On the Death of a Quack' (1–235) and 'The Quack and the Cobler' (Pforzheimer Misc. MS 197). The first 'was written on a quack Docter who came to Deeping' and the second Clare refers to as 'a true tale'.

ll. 679–84 Clare's poem 'The Village Doctress' contrasts with Dr Urine and this part of *The Parish*. See John Clare, *The Midsummer Cushion*, edited by Anne Tibble and R. K. R. Thornton (Manchester, 1979), pp. 143–9.

ll. 715–38 Compare these lines with Clare's prose passage 'Every farmer is growing into an orator and every village into a Forum of speech making and political squabbles . . .' ('John Clare' in *Oxford Authors*, p. 448) and Clare's letter to George Darley, 1830: 'How the times have altered the opinions and views of the people even here we have our villages mustering into parliments and our farmers puffing themselves up into orators and there is scarcley a clown in the village but what has the asumption to act the politician' ('John Clare' in *Oxford Authors*, p. 501).

l. 761 *the News*: a leading weekly newspaper published between 1805 and 1839.

l. 770 *Cobbets truth*: William Cobbett (1763–1835), popular journalist, originally a Tory, wrote from the radical viewpoint from 1804, playing an important political role as a champion of traditional rural England against the changes wrought by the Industrial Revolution. He wrote with vigour and sound sense on agricultural matters, but his honesty and shrewdness were marred by an arrogant and quarrelsome attitude which Clare deprecated.

l. 862 *'Pinks' or 'Blues'*: Tories or Whigs.

l. 907 *Burdett and Brougham*: Sir Francis Burdett (1770–1844), the most popular English politician of his day, entered the House of Commons in 1796. He made a name for himself by opposing the wars with France, and advocating parliamentary reform, Catholic emancipation, freedom of speech, prison reform, and other liberal measures.

Henry Brougham (1778–1868), Whig politician and law-reformer, was an important figure in the reforming movements of the time. His eloquence and boldness, though they lost him the favour of the crown, brought him the support of the people, and in the 1820s when he was advocating the total abolition of slavery and better education for the poor he became a popular idol. He was a practical man who struggled to put right the abuses which he saw around him.

l. 1056 *Dagons*: Dagon was the national deity of the ancient Philistines.

ll. 1064–5 Cf. Exodus 3:8.

l. 1075 *Moors new year*: Francis Moore, astrologer and quack physician, began, in 1699, an almanac forecasting the weather as a means of advertising his pills.

l. 1091 Oliver Goldsmith, 'And e'en his failings leaned to virtue's side', from 'The Deserted Village', line 164.

l. 1093 *'still small'*: cf. 'still small voice', 1 Kings 19:12.

ll. 1142–3 James Shirley, 'Only the actions of the just/Smell sweet, and blossom in their dust', from 'Ajax and Ulysses', 1659.

l. 1164 *Piering* = Peering. Clare seems to be saying that worth, like the sun, shines out upon, i.e. peers its influence on, the happy day.

l. 1203 Cf. Genesis 41.

l. 1208 *the village constable*: the village or parish constable was an officer of the parish or township appointed to act as conservator of the peace and to perform a number of public administrative duties in his district. See W. E. Tate, *The Parish Chest* (3rd edn, Cambridge, 1969).

l. 1219 *'beggars king'*: this title is repeated at line 1950.

l. 1220 *Overseers*: an overseer, short for Overseer of the Poor, was a parish officer appointed annually to perform various administrative duties mainly connected with the relief of the poor. The office was created by Act 43 Eliz. c. 2, and the duties were defined to include causing able-bodied paupers to work, giving relief to the disabled poor, putting poor children to work, apprenticing them, etc., and raising by rate the necessary funds for these purposes. See W. E. Tate, *The Parish Chest*.

l. 1230 *Parish Clerk*: Clare is given to making fun of parish officers, and that is not surprising when one remembers that his grandfather John Donald Parker, the schoolmaster of Helpston, seduced Clare's grandmother, Ann Stimson.

l. 1264 *Sancho of the magistrates*: Sancho Panza, the squire of Don Quixote in Cervantes' romance. A short pot-bellied rustic, full of common sense but lacking in spirituality, he became governor of Barataria. He rode upon an ass, Dapple, and was famous for his proverbs. Panza, in Spanish, means paunch – hence Sancho Panza denotes a rough-and-ready justice of the peace.

ll. 1276–7 Samuel Butler's satirical poem 'Hudibras' appeared shortly after the Restoration and was set in the time of the Civil War, when people were massacring one another 'they knew not why'. Sir Hudibras, the grotesque and blustering knight of a hot-headed cause goes forth in company with his squire Ralph. The first is a Presbyterian, the second an Independent, and their continual arguing reflects an epoch when sect opposed sect in endless strife. Their relevance to Clare's theme is obvious.

ll. 1279–80 This was a practice followed in Helpston, since Clare mentions that it occurred in connection with his father Parker Clare. If the practice was general it seems to have evaded the notice of most historians of the Poor Law.

l. 1295 Cobbett has the following version in his *Political Register*: 'Set a beggar on horse-back, and he'll ride to the Devil'.

l. 1310 *Tyburn tree*: Tyburn was a place of public execution until 1784. It was situated at the junction of the present Oxford Street, Bayswater Road, and Edgware Road. Hence used allusively for the gallows. It was a common practice to publish broadsheets giving in ballad form the last words of hanged malefactors.

l. 1353 *parish vestrys*: the parish vestry was orginally the 'open' general meeting of rate-paying householders in a parish, usually in the vestry, later becoming the 'close' governing body of a parish, the members generally having a property qualification and being recruited more or less by co-option. Administration of the Poor Law was one of its main tasks.

l. 1400 *justice Terror*: a local magistrate and a Justice of the Peace. Mr Hopkinson of Morton was just such a figure, see *The Autobiographical Writings of John Clare*, pp. 121–3

l. 1411 *toll fees*: during the eighteenth century the number of turnpike trusts used by Parliament increased steadily until early in the nineteenth century they numbered 1,100, controlled 23,000 miles of roads and had in 1837 a toll revenue of one and a half million pounds per annum. There was at the time Clare was writing *The Parish* a turnpike road between Peterborough and the neighbouring village of Glinton.

l. 1427 *'the man in black'*: Clare may have been remembering the Man in Black in Goldsmith's 'Citizen of the World', a humorist, a man generous in the extreme, who wished to be thought of as a prodigy of parsimony.

ll. 1428–9, 1498–1507 We are sure Clare would have agreed with the following piece on Sunday observance which appeared in *Drakard's Stamford News* 23 May 1823: 'Three boys were placed in the stocks a few days since at Castor, near Peterborough, for *three* hours, for the enormous offence of *playing* with marbles on a Sunday. Here is truly an illustration of the worn-out and lying boast of the law "being the same for the prince and the peasant:" for while in London, streets are blocked up with impunity during the whole of a Sunday evening, by strings of carriages setting down their noble owners for an evening concert, where in pretty commixture perhaps Nancy Dawson and Handel's Hallelujahs float along the air, these poor lads, who are toiling all the week for their miserable *scale* allowance of 1s. 9d. or 2s. 6d., are not, on pain of a disgraceful exposure to their village neighbours, to think of any thing in the shape of recreation. Out upon such hypocritical cant.'

The *Stamford Mercury*, 31 March 1815, contains the following report: 'Four boys of Whaplode Drove were taken before the magistrates on Sunday se' nnight, for playing at marbles on that day: three of them were fined 6s. 8d. each, and the other was committed to prison for being impudent to the magistrates.'

l. 1485 Pope, *An Essay on Criticism*, line 215.

ll. 1584–1787 Clare in this section of *The Parish* follows closely his earlier poem 'The Vicar' (1821), but ll. 1584–7, 1600–1601, and 1692–3 are new.

ll. 1788–1831 Clare's poem 'The Workhouse Orphan' (Pierpont Morgan Library, MA 1320, pp. 78–84) contains a section on the lot of children in a workhouse:

> With Mary Lee the parish was my lot
> & its cold bounty all the friends I got
> Dragd from our childhoods pleasures & its plays
> We pind in workhouse sorrows many days
> Were many wants recievd their scant supply
> Were pity never came to check the sigh
> Save what laws force from tyrant overseers
> Whose bitter gifts was purchasd with our tears
> There ragd & starvd & workd beyond our powers
> We toild those hours you spend in gathering flowers
> Nor mothers smiles had we our toils to cheer
> But tyrants frowns & threatnings ever near
> Who beat enfeebld weakness many times
> & scoft misfortunes agonys as crimes
> While prides vain childern of a luckier race
> Were taught to shun our presence as disgrace
> Thus workhouse misery did we both abide
> Till our own strength its poverty supplyd
> & service freed us –

l. 1848 *Farmer Thrifty*: Clare writes in Pforzheimer Misc. MS 198–1: 'What changes has fashion made since it crept out of the great City into the Villages

it is some 50 years since Job Thrifty the last of the oppulent farmers of the old school flourished in his popularity who was a very rich, plain, and superstitious man whose enemys called him "Horse shoe Jack" from a failing he had in believing in witches and a practice which he indulged in of nailing old horse shoes about the thresholds of his house and stables to prevail as a spell against these nightly depredations . . .'

l. 1918 *up his sleeve to creep*: Clare uses the same phrase in 'My Mary':

> For theres none apter I believe
> At 'creeping up a Mistress' sleve'
> Then this low kindred stump of Eve
> My Mary

ll. 2068–97 Referring to his father, Clare writes in B 3–86: 'and as soon as he went to the parish for relief they came to clap the town brand on his goods and set them down in their parish books because he shoud not sell or get out of them

I felt utterly cast down for I coud not help them sufficient to keep them from the parish so I left the town and got work at Casterton with Gordon   I felt some consolement in solitude from my distress by letting loose my revenge on the unfeeling town officer in a Satire on the "Parish" which I forbore to publish after wards as I thought it . . .' See E. Robinson, *The Autobiographical Writings of John Clare*, p. 115. J. W. and A. Tibble in *The Prose of John Clare* (London, 1951) suggest in a footnote on p. 67 that 'the unfeeling town officer' is possibly 'Bumtagg the bailiff'.

l. 2129 *M* *Puff*: derived from Puff, the well-known character in Sheridan's *The Critic*, 1779, who reduced the gentle art of literary advertisement to regular rule and scientific method.

l. 2139 *tree of knowledge*: Genesis 2:9 and 12.

l. 2158 *Pharoahs kine*: Genesis 41.

l. 2159 *Sir Walter*: Sir Walter Scott.

l. 2196 The more usual version of the proverb is 'If the cap fit, wear it'.

Glossary

awthorn, *n.*, hawthorn

bantum, *n.*, bantam, cock
borough town, *n.*, a town which is a
   borough
burthend, *adj.*, loaded, burdened

cast, *v.*, cast off
cavil, *n.*, specious objection
childern, *n.*, children
choak, *v.*, choke
Ciceronian, *adj.*, resembling Cicero
   in eloquence
cloaths, *n. pl.*, clothes
clown, *n.*, rustic
controul, *n.*, control
cot, *n.*, cottage
creep up a sleeve, get into favour
   with, ingratiate
crimp, *v.*, wrinkle
crumble, *n.*, crumb

deserving, *adj.*, deserving of
   punishment
distress, *v.*, use the legal right of
   distraint

earnest, *n.*, money paid as instalment,
   especially to confirm contract
eke, *v.*, stretch out, increase
encrease, *v.*, increase

gaud, *n.*, gaudy show
gaul, *v.*, gall
grain, *n.*, larger branch of a tree,
   bough
grave, *v.*, engrave
green sickness, *n.*, anaemic disease

mostly affecting young women,
giving a pale or greenish tinge to
the complexion
grub, *v.*, dig up, uproot

heer, *v.*, hear
heir, *v.*, inherit
hight, *adj.*, called, named

lawn, *n.*, fine linen
loath, *adj.*, Clare's spelling of loth
loose, *v.*, Clare's spelling of lose
lurcher, *n.*, used by Clare in the
   double sense of dog for game and
   swindler

mort, *n.*, lot, large number
motley, *adj.*, dressed in various
   colours

near, *adv.*, Clare's spelling of ne'er

outherod, *v.*, outdo Herod
   (represented in medieval Mystery
   Plays as a blustering tyrant)
oratorial, *adj.*, oratorical

parrarell, *n.*, parallel, equal
patronizer, *n.*, patron
pelf, *n.*, money, ill-gotten gains
presevere, *v.*, persevere
printers devil, *n.*, errand-boy in a
   printing office
puff, *n.*, advertisement containing
   exaggerated or false praise

racket, *n.*, gaiety, social excitement
racket, *v.*, live a gay life

ramping, *adj*., coarse, luxuriant

roast, *n*., roost

Rotten borough, *n*., one of the
boroughs which, before the passing
of the Reform Bill in 1832, were
found to have so decayed as no
longer to have a real constituency

roughish, *adj*., roguish

rout, *n*., party, social gathering

runnel, *n*., stream, brook, rill

ryhme, *v*., rhyme

schollard, *n*., an intentionally
ignorant version of 'scholar'

scource, *n*., source

scrat, *v*., scratch

sherk, *n*., shark

sink, *n*., pool or pit formed in the
ground for receiving waste water,
sewage, etc.; cesspool

snob, *n*., colloquialism for shoemaker

speed, *v*., thrive

stickle, *v*., stick

sware, *v*., swear

teaze, *v*., irritate

then, *conj*., Clare's spelling of than

tother, *n*., the other

town, *n*., often used by Clare for
village

tythe, *n*., tithe

usuage, *n*., usage

wanting, *adj*., needy

were, *adv*., Clare's usual spelling of
where

wether, *conj*., whether

whimsey, *n*., whim

wipe away, *v*., clear away, put aside,
remove

yclypd, *adj*., called by the name of